Mist on the Window

By

Susan Thomas-Czarnecki

Illustrations by
Magdalena Pytka

Edited by
Mary Linn Roby

authorHOUSE®

AuthorHouse™ UK Ltd.
500 Avebury Boulevard
Central Milton Keynes, MK9 2BE
www.authorhouse.co.uk
Phone: 08001974150

First published by AuthorHouse 2/26/2010

ISBN: 978-1-4490-8153-9 (sc)

This book is printed on acid-free paper.

For Anna and John

Contents

1

Mr. Kramer Locked Up

"You didn't?" said Kathy, her eyes as big as Mum's new dinner plates.

"I did!" answered Susan, proudly sticking out her chin.

"You really did it?" asked Kathy, clearly awestruck. "I wish I'd been there. What did he say?"

Susan chuckled. "He just sort of spluttered and muttered something about seeing the headmistress!"

"Gosh, you're so brave. I wish I could shut *our* French teacher in the cupboard!"

"Silly! You don't do French yet."

"I'm not silly," Kathy retorted crossly, "but it would be kind of fun. Maybe we could shut all the teachers in the cupboard!"

Mum came into the kitchen where the girls were eating their usual bowls of soggy cornflakes, flustered as she was most mornings when she found her two daughters dawdling yet again.

"Are you two still here?" she demanded. "You should be on your way to school. Peter, come down this instant!" she called to her youngest.

"I can't find my red thockth to go with my jumper!" Peter yelled from upstairs.

"Guess what Susan did in school yesterday!" Kathy said.

Susan glared at her sister. "Don't you dare!" she threatened.

"Now, you two, get a move on or you'll both be late for school. Your school blazer is hanging in the cloakroom, Susan. Kathy, Daddy will take you to school today. Peter, where are you?"

And so yet another school day began.

Susan wondered whether the headmistress had heard about her escapades in the French lesson the previous day. The girls in her class had all agreed that it was Mr. Kramer's fault because he really shouldn't have sniggered behind his coffee cup at Jenny who was trying to say "methee bookoop." Jenny couldn't help speaking that way. Susan wondered if her brother, with his serious lisp, ever had the same problems in school. If he did, Peter would make a joke out of it as he did with everything. Not Jenny though. She was more like Kathy – shy, and very often close to tears.

Well, Mr. Kramer had got what he deserved, Susan decided, though she wasn't sure that Miss Braybern, the headmistress, would see it that way. If Kathy were to tell Mum or Dad about Susan shutting Mr Kramer in the cupboard for the entire lesson, she knew there would be major trouble!

As a result, she walked to school very slowly almost jumping out of her skin when her friend Helena tapped her on the shoulder. And, when Mr Kramer walked past during break, she pretended to be reading her geography book. Actually, she quite liked French and she and Kathy always had great fun pretending they were French tourists when they were shopping together.

But better even than speaking gobbledy gook with Parisian accents in Tesco, was playing practical jokes on unsuspecting teachers and neighbours. She had never dreamt that one day she might get caught. But today – well today might just see her in front of the old battle axe and that would not be good, particularly since, according to Dad, she was supposed to be "keeping a low profile", a phrase he had used on countless occasions since he discovered that his eldest daughter had passed the entrance exam to the Girl's Grammar School. Susan still wasn't sure what a "profile" was but she knew she should try to be "good", at least – which, to her, meant being "boring".

Dad was the headmaster of the boy's school the other side of town and Susan realized now why she should have "kept the low profile" he was always talking about! Headmasters have meetings with headmistresses, which was why, on this particular morning, she saw him stride into her headmistress's office at lunch time.

Actually, the P.E. lesson, straight after lunch, took her mind off the imminent danger. It was the dreaded cross country again. Helena, Gemma and Susan -"the

4

terrible triplet" as some teachers called them - usually cut through the housing estate to avoid having to run three miles to Maiden Castle. This time Susan suggested, to the surprise of the other two, that they run the full distance.

"Are you crazy?" said Gemma, who refused to run anywhere unless it was away from a spider. "My legs won't take me that far!"

"Ow...agh... I've got ...cramp in my ...leg!" Helena plonked herself down on the grass verge outside the local fish and chip shop. "I can't go any further," she groaned.

"Get up, Helee," Susan pleaded. "Angela has overtaken us. We always get back to school before Angela. Oh, no. I don't believe it. Miss Planter is coming."

"You've gotta be kidding," said Gemma, helping Helena stagger to her feet. "She always drives her car. What's she doing running?"

Sure enough, Miss Planter came jogging past them at an even pace, encouraging each of the girls she passed with a smile and a, "See you at the gate."

As she passed Susan and her friends, however, her expression changed.

"Will you come to see me in my office when you get back to school, Susan," she said, frowning.

"Do you think she's been talking to Mr Kramer?" Gemma asked quietly when Miss Planter went jogging on.

"Oh, come on. You know as well as I do that sport and I just don't mix! Playing hockey in school time is one thing, but you won't get me giving up my Saturday afternoons to play against bunches of sissies. That's when I get to go with my dad to rugby matches with the boys from his school."

"You're so lucky!" Helena exclaimed. "When are you going to invite us, anyway?"

"I'll talk to Dad! Hey, we'd better go. History starts in five minutes and I've got to get my books from the changing room. See you up in class."

The history lesson dragged but, for once, Susan was not at all happy to hear the bell for the end of school. She was able to delay the inevitable by escorting first Helena and then Gemma home and although Dad never usually got home much before the six o'clock news, today she noticed his bike was already propped up outside the back door as she walked slowly up the driveway.

"Where have you been?" Mum asked her, " I was just about to call Gemma's mother to see where you'd got to. Oh, Darly. Could you lift the pan down for me? No – the other one," she added, turning her attention to Dad, who, having provided her with the necessary assistance, sat down, poured himself a cup of tea and opened the newspaper.

"How's my girl?" he asked, catching Susan round the waist as she hurried past him, desperate to escape the kitchen unnoticed and unquestioned.

"Fine, Dad. Um, Helena was asking if she could come with us to a match one Saturday?" Susan said, hoping to distract him from whatever he may have heard at school. "Could she?"

"There isn't a match tomorrow, Suz. Maybe next Saturday. We'll see."

And although Susan knew from experience that "We'll see" was a way of saying "No," she wasn't going to try and twist his arm at this moment. When he asked her to bring him his briefcase which he'd left under the stairs, she wanted to blurt out that she was sorry, that she would apologize to Mr. Kramer, that she would try to be good and "keep a low profile".

When she returned to the kitchen, both Mum and Dad were sitting at the table and Susan knew she was probably in big trouble. Neither Kathy, who was at her athletics club, nor Peter, who always played with Ben on Fridays after school, was home to help her by interrupting and distracting them.

"Sit down, Susan," Dad said. "We'd like to talk to you."

"Don't look so worried, dear," Mum said, when Susan did as she was told. "You're not in trouble. Unless there's something you want to tell us, of course." And then, when Susan didn't answer, "Okay Darly, why don't you ask her?"

"Thanks, Tunky."

Susan took a deep breath and let out a very long sigh. The fact that they were using their special pet names for each other was a good sign. She didn't need to worry, after all. But why all this business of asking her to sit down in front of them if they were not going to tell her off?

"Mum and I have been talking," Dad was saying, "and we think it's time that we asked you if, rather than going with us on holiday this summer, you might prefer to go somewhere with your friends. After all, you *are* almost fourteen and you've been working really hard in school this year. So what about it? We've spoken to Mrs Arneat and she's quite happy for Helena to do something with you?"

Oh, the thrill! Susan could hardly believe her ears. All her friends in school were going to exotic places like France and Spain and she had been wanting to ask her mum and dad if they would let her do something special this summer. But she knew that her parents were not the same as other people's. These were parents who did not allow her to use a calculator during maths exams or computers when doing homework, saying that she needed to use her head and that she would thank them one day! These were parents who said that mobile phones were a way of preventing young people from saving and these were parents who disapproved of discos and pyjama parties and carnivals, and... Well, they were strict, that's all! So, to hear them say that she could go away for the summer without them just didn't fit the picture!

"Oh, thank you, thank you, thank you!" and jumping up, she gave them both a big hug, spilling dad's tea in the process and banging her knee on her chair.

"Go on, get yourself out of your school uniform and come down for some tea. We'll talk about the details later." Mum, rose to finish boiling some eggs and Dad returned to his newspaper. Susan couldn't wait till Kathy and Peter came home to gloat! Gosh, they would be so jealous!

But, as it turned out, there was no chance of telling them anything.

"I met Seline! I met Seline!" Kathy cried as she raced into the living room where Dad was watching the news.

"Come and sit beside me and tell me all about it," he said tapping the seat next to him.

Susan knew that her sister had met Seline Drane at the sport's centre and had been given some tips on how to improve her hurdling technique by one of England's brightest new stars and a potential Olympic contestant. Now Dad, clearly impressed, wanted to hear all the details.

Later, when Kathy had gone upstairs it was Peter's turn, although his took the form of racing round and round the room with the belt from his dressing gown shouting, "Yippee, yahoo" as he tried to lasso dad and tie him to the chair.

"I think it's time for your bath, Peter," Mum said when Dad finally breathed a deep sigh. "Your poor father is trying to watch the news. Let's leave him in peace. I'm sure he'll come and hear you read a chapter of *Cowboy Jim and the ranchers* later if you ask him nicely."

"Oh, will you, Dad?" Peter shouted. "I got an "A" in thchool for reading today!"

"Of course I will. Call me after your bath and I'll be up."

And so the moment for Susan to gloat aloud passed by and it was not until the following morning, when they were all sitting together at the table for a very late breakfast, Mum, still in her pyjamas as usual, and Dad, unshaven, and drinking his only cup of coffee of the week, that the topic of holidays came up again.

2

Dilemma. Teignmouth or Rome?

"Peter, do you think you could possibly stop racing round for just a brief moment? I'm sure Ivor the engine could do with a break."

"Peter, you heard what your father said." Mum joined in the attempt to get Peter to stop charging round the room chugging and whistling like a steam train. Circling the kitchen table one more time, he eventually shunted to a halt.

"Psh – ti - koof, psh – ti – koof, oo oo at your thervith!" grinned the lively nine year old as he sat down with a "humph" on his chair next to Kathy. "What you thtaring at, thith?" asked Peter, his lisp always more pronounced when he was out of breath.

"How come boys can always do such good impersin... im- perso ..."

"Impersonations!" Mum prompted her.

"That was what I was saying - impers i whatsits of cars and things," continued Kathy. "My sounds always come out wrong."

"Mithyth Lithee thayth ith becauth we've got better imagination."

"You have not. I bet you can't write a poem about frogs like we had to in school last week," said Kathy with conviction.

"I bet you I could. Lithen..

There onth wath a frog called tattoo, who decided to go to the loo..."

"Peter, if you wouldn't mind! We are still at the table and we are waiting to talk to you. You and Kathy can make up frog poems when you get down."

"But the frog can't wait to go to..."

"Peter, enough is enough!" Dad was getting annoyed.

"By Joan V. Flaylor. A pink book on the second shelf!" Susan said quietly, though not quite quietly enough. Dad cast her a look which meant, "Don't you start, madam!" but she could not resist it having noticed a book by that title on his shelf just a couple of days before. Dad was so cute when he got cross.

He tried to look stern although there was always a smile at the corner of his mouth and a gleam in his eyes. Susan thought it might be a good thing if Peter calmed down, just in case!

"May I speak now?" asked Dad. No one dared to say anything so he continued.

"You may remember we told you at the end of our last summer holiday that the hotel in Teignmouth was closing down and that we wouldn't be able to go there again. Well, I've just had a very pleasant chat with the proprietor, Mr. James, and he informs me that they're going to be open for tourists this summer and that he's keeping our room for us in case we're interested in visiting again. But, of course, I told him I would have to ask you all first."

"It was very nice of him to call, Darly. I wonder what made him do that?" asked Mum, and Susan could see from the tears in her eyes that news of the hotel closing had deeply affected her.

"Well, I suppose we've been faithful over the years and he knows how disappointed we were when we heard the news," said Dad, quite clearly oblivious to the chaos that was going on around him as the three children, having been told to calm down just five minutes earlier were now jumping up and down and chanting "Teignmouth, Teignmouth! Here we come! here we come!" Kathy and Susan began to sing the song they had made up the year before as they had been crawling along the motor way in yet another traffic jam and before long the whole family had joined in.

We're off to see our hotel, the wonderful hotel of the South

Won't we have fun, as we play in the sun

And get sand in our toes and our mouths.

"That's not fair," Susan thought to herself, as Mum and Dad, making no effort to calm them down this time, left the kitchen their arms round each other. She hadn't had a moment to tell Kathy and Peter that Mum and Dad were going to let her go away with a friend in the summer. And now *they* were going to be going to Teignmouth, "Her Teignmouth".

She remembered how she had wept quietly in her bedroom the day she heard the hotel was to be closed. She loved Teignmouth. She had been going there ever since she was two years old and it had become as special to her as Gran and Grampa's garden with its intricate maze of stone paths weaving their way through little flower gardens with lavender scattered everywhere and lilac lining the wall or Granma's secret cupboard with the stairs hidden away that she waited to discover each time she went to Wales at Easter.

Even though she had never spent more than two weeks out of the year in Teignmouth, she only had to close her eyes to see the coloured lights twinkling in the evening, the pretty flower beds lining the promenade, the Ferry and Smuggler's Tunnel, the winding roads and fascinating little shops with souvenirs. She loved her hotel with the dark TV room and the secret corridors but most of all she loved being away from the town where she was known as the headmaster's daughter and was laughed at for playing the violin and going to church on Sundays.

Susan made up her mind there and then. She would give anything to go to Teignmouth again, even if it meant giving up the chance to be "independent".

3

Back in Devon

Monday saw Susan, Kathy and Peter back at school. The summer term was long. Interminably so. Mr Kramer remained watchful and on guard until the exams were out of the way and report cards written before handing in his notice. No one seemed to be sorry about his leaving, but everyone knew about what had happened to him, including the staff, and Susan heard that the other teachers had been warned to be on their guard as far as the terrible triplets were concerned.

Susan, Helena and Gemma were caught ambling through the housing estate and spent fifteen minutes of each P.E. lesson running round the tennis courts as a punishment. Kathy, on the other hand, ran for pleasure and finished the school term with flying colours by winning the county championships in both the 100 meter sprint and the hurdles. Peter continued to race everywhere except for the odd moments when he sat still to write his little ditties, one of which, a poem entitled *Under My Bed* won an award in the poetry competition in his school.

Susan enjoyed a moment of glory when she came top in her class in Latin but plummeted down to earth a few days later when the award was given to rival Kantina whose Italian mother just happened to be on the Board of Governors.

Out of school, boys continued to walk on the other side of the road whenever they saw the Thomas children coming, jeering "Walter Penguin's kids!" Susan vowed never to let on that her dad's initials W.M. did *not* stand for Walter Martin but for William Michael. At least "Walter's kids" was better than "Willie's kids!"

But the day eventually crept up on them. School actually did end and Susan, shoulders slouching and kicking stones, returned home to present her parents with a school report with a grade for behaviour that left a lot to be desired.

She hadn't told anyone that she was going to go on holiday with her mum and dad again this summer, suggesting instead that they might go abroad, perhaps even to California which, while not an elaborate lie was enough to keep the girls in her class wondering whether she might bump into film stars on the street. Helena had been disappointed to learn that Susan would not be going with her to Rome but even *she* did not know about Susan's decision to return to Teignmouth.

Finally the day arrived and they were off, Dad having shut the door to his study with a resounding click and smiling with satisfaction as he picked up their bags and told them to get in the car.

They had needed no persuasion, and now four hours later, Susan, who had been day dreaming, was astonished to find that they were there and that Dad was actually passing the end of the road with *Sweet Memories,* the quaint little sweet shop with her favourite liquorice allsorts and jelly babies in beautiful pink and green and yellow teddy bear-shaped jars as well as a tantalizing five-foot ice cream cone outside on the pavement, a perfect encouragement to go inside.

"Why have we stopped?" she asked.

"Don't tell me you've forgotten this place, Susan?" Mum exclaimed.

"No, of course I haven't forgotten!" Susan shouted trying to push Kathy's head out of the way so that she could get a better look. Look! there's Donna the sweetie lady."

"OW, stop it! I want to see as well, you know!"

"Are you all ready?" Dad said, slowing the car as he always did just before they turned the last corner before they reached the hotel.

Kathy and Susan cried "Yes!" in unison, and Peter, who had dozed off earlier, opened his eyes and shouted, "I CAN..."

"I CAN SEE THE SEA! I CAN SEE THE SEA! I CAN SEE THE SEA!" Kathy and Susan screamed. Mum glared at her girls. But it was a glare mixed with a grin. Susan knew that not even one of Mum's glares would be able to stop their thrill at this moment. And then the best moment of all. The hotel came into sight.

But Susan had no words to describe just how happy she felt so she sat still and quiet.

4

The Hotel

Dad parked round the back of the hotel in a dark car park, shadowy, because it was enclosed on one side by the back wall of the hotel with doors leading to the store rooms and the kitchen. Susan knew that because last year she had walked in when no-one was looking. She had not got far because a big fat man with a greasy apron, carrying a tray piled high with plates told her she shouldn't be there and asked where her parents were, before ushering her back out but not before she heard utensils clanging against the sides of saucepans and sizzling sounds. Somehow it wasn't a friendly place, smelling as it did of a mixture of yesterday's chips and cake and fresh bread and bleach. At all events, Susan wasn't keen to open that door again.

That was one side of the car park. The other side was just a high wall – no door, no windows, no roof. No way in and no way out. This year, Susan decided, she wanted to discover what was behind that wall.

"You're day dreaming again, Susan!" Mum said, handing Susan her big brown leather handbag, the one that had a secret pocket at the back that Mum didn't know Susan knew about. "Here, hold this."

Susan had found the pocket once when her mum had asked her to put her lipstick back in and to see if she could find her handkerchief. Mum rarely wore lipstick but she was always losing her hanky. If it wasn't tucked up a sleeve or in the waistband of her skirt it could have been anywhere. But it was *never* where she wanted it to be.

"Susan, will you please watch what you are doing?" she added as Susan took a step backward, blocking her way out of the car.

At that moment Dad came back with Kathy clinging to his arm, something she sometimes did when she was feeling shy. Give her a new place or a new face and she would go into her shell like the neighbour's tortoise. At other times she would shout in rage and run out of the room slamming the door behind her. But right now Dad was struggling to get the remaining luggage out of the car along with a nervous daughter. Handing Mum a small bag and manoeuvring Kathy to his left, he picked up the last suitcase and led the way to the hotel.

Susan held back, much in the same way as she used to when she would stay ten paces behind all of them during Sunday afternoon walks.

This was to be her private moment. She did not want to be asked how she felt or to hear "how lovely everything was" and "wasn't it grand to be back?"

The sea was just as she remembered – splashing playfully on the rust-coloured sand with children scampering to escape the waves. The seagulls were circling overhead, waiting for pieces of bread to be thrown in their direction and OH the smell – that faint smell of seaweed and the saltiness in the air carried in their direction by the breeze. There was often a gentle breeze here. But that was all Susan had time to notice because at that very moment they arrived at the wide stone steps leading up to the glass front doors, the bowl of water in its familiar spot just to the side and sand everywhere!

Oh, she was so glad that she had decided to come! Susan was sure that there would be happy days ahead.

5

Mrs. Gerty

"Oh, Darly we're back!" Mum was looking at Dad with that look in her eyes that made Susan think of those romantic moments in the movies when the princess gazes at the prince and the violins begin to play.

"Phuj!" Susan muttered under her breath, hoping that they wouldn't actually kiss one another right here in the reception hall with everyone looking. That would be so embarrassing. She was relieved when, at that precise moment, Dad was called over to the desk. Talk about being saved by the bell!

There was a skinny man standing behind the desk wearing a peculiar old-fashioned cream shirt with a massive collar and a wide blue and white striped tie, looking, Susan thought, as if he had walked out of one of the 1960's fashion magazines like Granma sometimes had lying around in her house. The previous two years there had been a skinny, very cross old lady named Mrs. Gerty behind the counter who always had her hair tied so tightly on the back of her head that it made her ears stick out and her eyes go skewiff. The girls used to call her "Mrs. Farty" until Dad had over-heard them giggling and said it wasn't nice to call people names.

"Come on, Bach, let's see if any of you remember the way." Dad spoke with a gentle lilt which comes from having spent his childhood and youth in a small Welsh mining village. He was holding the key to room number ten in his left hand, trying to juggle it with one of the suitcases and pointing with his nose to the stairs. The stairs were so wide that all of the family could have walked up them hand in hand and there would still have been room for people to pass by.

"Shall I carry the picnic basket?" Susan offered, hoping that they would say "No, it's okay, dear. Just you run along ahead." But instead her Mum said, "That would be lovely, Suz. Thank you and could you come and walk with Kathy as well?"

Susan gritted her teeth. There went her chance of dashing up the stairs first and grabbing the bed next to the window... unless... She had a brainwave. Kathy was a budding athlete, always coming first in the 100 metres sprint– oh, except that time that Jennifer Plain pushed her at the start! The PE teacher announced in assembly one morning, as she handed Kathy with yet another diploma, that she would "go far".

"Kiff Sticks," Susan said, "let's see if I can beat you this time." Not surprisingly it was the right bait to use.

"Wait a minute, my shoe lace is undone."

"I'll do it for you" Susan put the basket down, did up Kathy's shoe lace whereupon, before she knew what was happening, her sister called out, "Ready, steady, go...." and disappeared round the first corner. Having been caught off guard, Susan, who wasn't about to be left stranded at the bottom of the stairs, hurtled up the first flight, round the bend, straight into the outstretched arms of Nanny.

"Well, well, well," she said stretching out her arms in welcome, a plump lady with rosy cheeks, wearing a flowery apron over a white cotton blouse and flowing skirt. "If it isn't the Thomas family. Back again are you, my sweetie? Now I know we're going to have a sunny week! Just a word of advice. Mrs Gerty is standing on the landing and I don't think she'll take too kindly to a young lady frightening her Paddy. Now run along there's a good girl —no, silly me, I mean walk! I'll be seeing you in the playroom no doubt unless, of course, you're too big to visit with me this year!"

And with that, Nanny winked at Susan, tapped her on her bottom, and walked off down the stairs humming happily to herself.

It had been good of Nanny to warn them, Susan thought, but she could tell from the expression in Mrs. Gerty's eyes that it was too late. Above them on the landing, that don't-mess-with-me, skinny woman was wearing her usual costume, a knee-length, heavy grey dress tied at the waist with an unattractive fraying, black material belt which made her look like an empty sack of coal. Her stockings had a ladder creeping up the bony shin of her left leg and her hair was, just as Susan always remembered it, tied back tightly in a bun at the nape of her long neck, stretching her face so tightly across her cheek bones that it was possible to work out what her skull looked like. In her arms, she was holding a heavy, old cat who must be Paddy. He looked like he would have preferred to be lying in front of a warm fire rather than being pinned to this flat – bosomed lady. Kathy was looking at the cat rather than at Mrs Gerty and was clearly trying hard to hold back the tears.

"WHAT IS THE WORLD COMING TO ? .... I WON'T HAVE CHILDREN RUNNING IN MY HOTEL.... YOU COULD HAVE KNOCKED ME OVER. WHERE ARE YOUR MUM AND DAD?.... I'LL HAVE A WORD WITH THEM, YOU MARK MY WORDS..... YOU WON'T HEAR THE LAST OF THIS.... THIS WOULD NOT HAVE HAPPENED IN MY DAY. LITTLE GIRLS WERE TO BE SEEN AND NOT HEARD!"

Puffing and panting she stormed off, clutching the poor cat.

"I hope it scratches your eyes out and I wish we *had* knocked you over," Susan muttered under her breath, but just loudly enough for Kathy to hear.

"You don't mean that, do you?" Kathy said, looking shocked.

"Yes, I do. She's always been mean to us and I intend to get her back – I don't know how yet but we've got two weeks to come up with a plan. Are you with me?"

"Yes, I'm standing right next to you," said Kathy, a little bemused.

"No, I mean do you want to help me think up a trick to play on Farty?"

"Yes, okay!" Susan could see that Kathy's mind was already beginning to tick.

"Come on," she said, "I can hear Mum and Dad coming. Wipe your face and let's pretend nothing has happened. Here's our room!"

Pushing the door slightly ajar, they peeked inside and found, to their great relief, that everything was just as they had left it the year before, the beds, the curtains, the sink.

And especially the view of the sea from the window beside the bed that Susan always claimed for her own.

Now, at last, they had really arrived, and their adventure could begin.

6

The Window

Dad came into view first, carrying the picnic basket which, Susan , in her excitement had left at the foot of the stairs, apparently having failed to meet Mrs. Gerty on his way up. Or, if he had, he was going to choose another moment to comment on the encounter.

"Well, girls I see you have good memories!" he said cheerfully. "Go on in!" And so they did just that, slowly at first and then with a "yippee!" Susan skipped over to the bed by the furthest wall, the one next to the window, and pressed her nose against the glass. To the right she saw the steps leading down to the beach and in the distance, further down the promenade – the Grand Pier, beyond which, silhouetted against the blue sky was Ness Head. She would have liked to have been able to see the Parson's railway tunnel, too, but that was hidden away to the left, round several serpentine bends. Besides, she wasn't going to be allowed to spend many moments gazing through the window. Mum arrived at that moment with Peter in tow, determined, as always, to unpack and get the room looking as much like home as possible and as equally determined not to be disturbed while she did so.

"Susan, why don't you and Kathy and Peter go down to the play room," she said. "We have about an hour before tea time and it'll give me chance to get things sorted out."

"Okay, Mum," the children replied in unison, darting out through the door before she could change her mind and ask them to help her with the unpacking.

"Girls!" called Dad, as they were about to shut the door behind them.

"Here we go," Susan said to Kathy with a sigh. "He did meet Mrs. Gerty, after all. Now we're in for it!"

"Don't be tempted to go exploring by yourselves, will you?" he said instead. "We'll be down once we've unpacked and we'll take you over to the beach. Make sure you go straight to the playroom, right?"

"We're not babies!" said Kathy as they heard the door click shut. "What do we want to go the playroom for? Can't we go up to the top landing instead? You promised to take us this year, Susan."

"Kathy, you heard what Dad said. Let's just do it on this occasion. We can always sneak out of the room when they are down in the lounge this evening!"

"Can I come too?" asked Peter, who was clearly fed up of being left out of all the fun.

"Only if you're good!" Susan was in charge now. As usual, she enjoyed the feeling of power she had over her younger brother. Oh, this was going to be great!

"Come on, both of you," she said. "It's okay, Kathy. You can relax now. Mrs. Gerty hasn't spoiled out holiday yet, and in fact, she might just provide us with some fun," Susan added with a grin.

Kathy looked as relieved as Susan felt as they walked down the stairs like real ladies with a, "Come on, slow coach" to Peter who didn't take long to catch up and overtake them.

The playroom door was closed and Nanny, who was jiggling a small child on her knee, beckoned to the children.

"Here we go," Susan said. "She's bound to tell us how much we've grown and ... don't we look like Mum!"

"So, who's this smart young gentleman you've brought with you?" Nanny exclaimed. "My, my, how you've all grown and you, young lady, you're more like your mum every time I see you!"

Kathy chuckled, and Susan grimaced, but Peter, as usual, was everywhere. Not much had changed. Toy cars were strewn everywhere, boys of all shapes and sizes were charging around pretending to be fire engines and helicopters, a small group of girls sat on the floor playing a game of snakes and ladders, and yet others were waiting their turn to go in the crazy see-saw which swivelled round and round as well as going up and down and made you want to be sick. Susan was glad her bottom was too big to squeeze into it this year although normally she was very conscious of her figure. When Peter charged past them making a "brrrrrrr.....brrrrrrrrr sounds, it occurred to her that perhaps they could get *him* to go in it.

Leaving Peter now galloping round the room with a new friend both 'eeee haaaing' and Kathy chatting to Nanny about hurdling, Susan excused herself politely as she had been taught to and walked over to the window overlooking the beach.

As she approached the window it clouded over as if she were breathing too hard and was misting it all up which was strange because all the others were perfectly clear. Looking back over her shoulder she could see Kathy still talking animatedly and showing Nanny her shin, which she had cut badly in her last hurdles race. Peter had decided to sit for a moment and was pushing a matchbox car under Nanny's leg.

When Susan looked back at the window the mist, or fog or whatever it was, had become even thicker. Without thinking too much about it Susan wiped the pane with her hand and looked out at her second most favourite place in Teignmouth .

She would have been looking at the beach if she could have seen it but there was nothing there. Nothing at all.

It was as if someone had painted the glass black. But it wasn't black it was just empty - a bit like being shut in the end of hall cupboard back home where there were no lights, no gap under the door – no nothing. Very, very slowly something strange began to happen.

Right in the middle of the nothingness the black began to turn grey and then golden. But still no beach. Susan rubbed her eyes. Standing absolutely still, she saw that something was swirling around outside.

It was as if all the sand on the beach had been thrown up in the air by an angry giant and was trying desperately to find a place to settle again. The sand began to mix with the frenzied seagulls overhead, being thrown this way and that by an invisible wind.

Suddenly from out of the chaos of twisting sand and screeching seagulls rose a ... a....a *hand*, reaching up higher and higher as if trying to reach for something or for someone,

As the hand came closer, she found herself reaching out for it, not wanting to touch but at the same time not wanting *not* to touch.

When their fingers touched on either side of the glass, Susan began to feel afraid. And then, suddenly, it all vanished. The sand. The seagulls. Everything was gone!

Susan was left with her hand on the glass, her breathing hard and fast and there, where the hand had been just seconds before was Teignmouth beach. Now the scene was a happy one again. Small children escaping excitedly from the gently lapping waves, relaxed parents drinking cold coffee from sandy thermos flasks and the curious, seagulls playing *Catch the Bread* or *Tap the Mussel* – a comic dance they performed by hopping round a shellfish, picking it up and smashing it on the promenade, running away if someone dared to get too close and then creeping back when the coast was clear. This was the scene Susan had always loved so much and now it had been spoiled by – by what she couldn't say.

"What's wrong, Susan?" Kathy asked as she joined Susan at the window. "You look like you've seen a ghost!"

"I... I... everything's... fine." Susan answered, her thoughts miles away. She wasn't easily frightened, unless it was by something like Dad walking into the headmistress's office. But this – well this was something different. Something she couldn't explain. Something she didn't want to explain.

"What - what do you say about trying to get Peter in the see-saw then!"

"Oh, yes, let's!" Kathy cried, grabbing Peter as he raced by them. But Susan didn't laugh hysterically like Kathy when Peter, his eyes bulging, his cheeks turning a strange greenish colour, began to yell, "Get me out, get me out! I'm going to be thick!"

No doubt Nanny noticed that her favourite summer visitor was not her usual, cheerful self but instead of asking her what was up, like most grown-ups do, she took hold of Susan's arm gently, plopped her down in a chair, put the baby she had been playing 'giddy-up' with firmly on her lap and with a sensitive, "There, there, my child, you just rock Janet on your lap for me, will you, while

I go and tend to your wee brother!" Unfortunately for Peter, the girls' idea of seeing him squirm in the notorious see-saw had ended as it had been known to before, with Peter's sausage and baked bean dinner splat right in the middle of a small group of boys who had until then been playing quite happily with their little cars.

"Yuck, ugh, phew!" The room was amok with kids trying to escape the mess. Poor Peter, he didn't look terribly cheerful! And Susan grinned in spite of herself, relieved to find herself back in the present and soon she found herself chanting her Grampa's famous "one-two-three-whoops" as she pretended to drop the unsuspecting little girl on the floor. Janet, a sweet, curly blond-haired little bundle giggled with glee and yelled, "More, more, more," to which Susan consented, her own love of children making her present baby-sitting job a pleasure rather than a chore.

"One-two-three – whoops!" It was as she was pretending to drop Janet for what must have been the hundredth time that Mum and Dad walked through the door. Luckily for the girls, Peter's face had returned to its normal colour, windows had been opened to let fresh air into the room and the floor had been lemon-bleached. Children were scampering everywhere again and Susan and Kathy were saved the embarrassment of having to explain themselves.

"Bye, Nanny," Peter said when Dad called, "Come on, you three!" Kathy just smiled and Susan, well Nanny took Janet from her and whispered, "It'll be alright lovey, just you see! Smile now deary! There you go! What about helping me with Janet again some time?"

"I'd like that!" Susan said, smiling, but as she turned round to walk out through the playroom door she glanced at the window – now clear and shining with a rosy tint in the evening sunlight.

7

So - Parents Know Everything!

Tea time was not uneventful. Peter chatted the entire time, about his new friend Jeremy and the remote control car that he had discovered in the corner of the playroom, hidden out of sight.

"Itth even got a thiren, which ith tho loud you have to put your fingerth in your earth."

"Don't you think that maybe Nanny hid it on purpose?" asked Mum, and Susan realized that she was rather worried that her youngest was going to prove a challenge for Nanny this year.

"No, itth great. I chathed Jeremy around the playroom with it and he had to thtand on the chair to get away and the chair fell over but heeth ok and......"

"Don't let me hear that you are being a nuisance, my lad," interrupted Dad "try and keep a low....."

".....profile." Susan finished the sentence for him, grinning as he turned to her with a confused expression.

"It seems, my dear, that your 'keeping a low profile' has led you into some very interesting scrapes!"

Susan did not know what to say to her father. Clearly he had heard about Mr. Kramer after all.

"Parents are not quite as daft as you may think, my dear," he told her. "They tend to know rather more than they let on. But with your exam courses beginning next term it might be advisable for you to pay rather more attention to your books than your favourite pastime which appears to be keeping your teachers on their toes, or rather in cupboards!"

Dad always sounded so posh when he talked but with his gentle lilting Welsh accent it was a pleasure to listen to him – even when he *was* being cross. Susan blushed. He did not seem terribly angry. But, if he had known about it all along, why hadn't he told her off before?

Mrs. Gerty's appearance on the scene helped to change the subject. Even Mum and Dad sometimes laughed together about how cross she always was and the children had once overheard them talking about her "unfulfilled ambition" and "ending up on the shelf" though, as parents, they were always quick to correct their children if *they* made fun of her. They had not yet quite grasped why it was that adults could say and do things that children couldn't and Peter especially was still at the stage of learning that his shouting at them when *he* was angry was not permitted while their shouting at him when *they* were angry apparently was.

Farty Gerty
wearing a dress
not very pretty
she's really a me...

"PETER!" Mum didn't want Mrs. Gerty coming over to them on their first evening any more than the children did, and while she would normally have laughed at Peter's rhymes, she didn't think that now was the time or the place to be overheard. Sadly it was too late. Mrs. Gerty's hearing was acute.

"I wanted a word, Mrs. Thomas," she said, biting off each word. " Please ask your children to refrain in future from charging up the stairs and I would appreciate it if you would ensure that they keep their voices down. I can't abide children who shout." And with that she strode off leaving both Mum and Dad simply looking at each other and then at the children in turn.

"You heard what she said," Dad said a minute later. "Girls, may I suggest you keep out of Mrs. Gerty's way this holiday, and Peter...?"

"Yeth, Dad?"

"You may want to compose your – poetry in the privacy of your own room. For your own sake!"

"Yeth, Dad!"

That evening brought the sparkle back into Susan's eyes. Oh, how those children laughed and shouted and enjoyed their first few moments of freedom. The sand was warm between their toes. Even Dad took his shoes and socks off. It was so lovely seeing him out of his study. Teignmouth always created new memories for them, and as if they were all thinking the same thought, they began to sing their family song.

We're a happy family,
Yes, a happy family
And we live at the end of Herringston Road
Susan and Kathy, nothing could be sweeter
And funny little Mum and Dad
Whoops – and Peter

Susan, halfway through the song began to look round her hoping that no one was watching. She really was getting too old for this and, when Mum asked her to link arms with her and do Mother Macree, she excused herself saying she had eaten too much toast at tea time and that her tummy was hurting. So, Mum joined hands behind her back with Kathy instead and skipped on ahead with a cheerful "Mother Macree went out to tea, shut the door and turned the key." The first attempt saw them turning round and getting all tangled up.

"Susan, come and show Kathy how to do this!"

"No way, Mum," Susan protested. At almost fourteen years of age she most certainly was not going to be seen skipping with her mummy! Instead she strolled alongside Peter. "I'm sorry we made you go in the seesaw Peter. It was really mean! Will you forgive me?"

"Yeh, all right. It wath really weird though. My head almotht fell off! I did make a meth, didn't I?"

"I'm just glad Mum and Dad didn't come in earlier. What would they have said?"

"Probably 'Thuthan, I thought you were a rethponthible young lady." Peter sounded so convincing in his mimicking of dad that Susan exploded and pushed Peter just a little too hard. Both of them ended up in a heap in the sand. It went everywhere, in their hair, up noses, down necks, but neither of them minded.

Thand, thand, everywhere.
In my nothe and in my hair.
Down my back and in my ear-th ....
tickling like little thpearth

"Peter, I think you'll be a famous poet one day!" said Susan, when she could get her breath back. Oh, it was good to laugh.

None of the children minded going to bed that evening. Peter fell asleep quickly and was soon making snuffling noises. As for Kathy, she tried to get Susan to think up some good pranks to play on Mrs. Gerty until

Susan managed to convince her that she was enjoying reading her book, after which Kathy eventually drifted off.

Quietly putting her book aside, Susan pulled the covers over her head and dozed off into a dream world crowded with teachers, seagulls pecking at their heads, clamouring to be let out of cupboards, and sand everywhere as an eventful day was followed by a restless night.

8

Steven's Back

Kathy was the first to wake up the next morning.

"Get up, you sleepy heads!" she cried, as she jumped from her bed to Peter's and then to Susan's landing with a thud right on her sister's tummy.

"Ugh! Get off, you heavy oaf. It's the middle of the night! Go back to sleep."

"It's not. Look the tractor's cleaning the beach already. Maybe it's Crazy Bucket-Chomping Harry! Remember him eating our bucket last year?" Susan remembered all right. All three of them had seen the bucket that Peter had left behind him disappearing into the tractor's jaws. Ever since then he'd been Bucket-chomping Harry.

"I wonder what he's going to eat this year!!" said Susan, yawning and pulling her blanket up under her chin. "Ow! You have got your knee stuck in my you-know-what! Ow! Get off."

"If you two can't you talk a little quieter you'd better go down to the dining room and see what's for breakfast."

Mum rolled over and disappeared in a pile of pillows including the one she always brought hers with her so that she could sleep in the car, with her feet up on the dashboard, skirt rolled up round her thighs and head comfortably propped up against the window.

Kathy, who was clearly intent on getting everyone up, grabbed a handful of Susan's blanket and tugged. Susan held on for dear life but Kathy was determined, so determined that Susan landed on her bottom on the hard, wooden floor.

"I'll get you," she hissed. "You wait and see." But Kathy was sprinting for the door, dragging her trousers on as she went, apparently forgetting that she was still wearing her pretty pink Barbie nightshirt only to return a few seconds later, letting the door slam behind her with a bang loud enough to wake Peter.

"GIRLS!"

"Sorry, Dad!" Kathy gasped and Susan saw that she was deathly pale.

Peter sat bolt upright in bed. "Where am I? What happened? Ith Laura Okay?"

"Laura, again. You're not going to tell us that you were dreaming about your friend's pet hamster again. We're in Teignmouth now. Anyway shut up. Kathy, what's wrong?"

"You won't believe it, even if I tell you," Kathy whispered with a look of absolute horror.

"It can't be that bad," Susan said putting on her slippers and wrapping her dressing gown tightly around her as she pushed Kathy away from the door and opened it a crack.

"Out of my way girlth. Thith ith a job for revolver Joe!" Peter said, sauntering past them, his hands on his hips, cowboy style, to poke his head out cautiously, as though the enemy was waiting outside.

"Oh, thith ith funny! He announced, turning to them with a grin. "Haa, haa...oh, it hurth. Thteeveeth back! Oh, my darling Kathy. I'm back, marry me!"

"Be quiet," Susan told him. "It isn't funny. Did you actually see Steven, Kathy?"

"...........................no............it was his ....dad..... and ....they've got the room......opposite ours. Our holiday's going to be a disaster."

"Remember hith red woolly jumper?" Peter demanded. "Do you think he'll be wearing it thith year too? Ooh, and that dithgusting thick, green thlimy bogey which he thneezed all over Kathy'th thleeve!"

"*Peter, you are not helping!*" Susan felt as worried as Kathy looked. If Steven really was here they wouldn't have a minute to themselves. "Peter, this really is a matter of life or death. Can you walk down to the bathroom and pretend you are Revolver Joe or, even better Pistol Pete and see is Steven really *is* in the hotel?"

"What will you give me if I do?"

"I'll buy you some Herbert Lemons," Susan told him.

"Ok, I'll do it, but it's got to be a big bag."

"What are you all whispering about over there?" Mum asked sleepily.

"Um..... nothing, Mum," Susan told her. "Go on Peter. And try to keep a low profile."

"You mean I've got to crawl like thith?" Peter said, getting down on all fours.

"No, you idiot! It's just something Dad says sometimes." Susan had a picture of her French teacher peering through the single pane of the French lab cupboard door. "Go on, get a move on"

"Okay, don't get your knickerth in a twitht!" And with that Peter crept sideways out of the door.

"We'd better get some clothes on, Kathy," Susan whispered.

"But if he's here, what are we going to do?"

"We'll work something out. Maybe we could get Mum and Dad to take us on the ferry to Shaldon today so that he won't see us on the beach."

"Can you ask them? They'll listen to you. *Please Susan.*"

"I'll try, I promise." Susan was only two years older than her sister, but at that particular moment, she felt the weight of the world on her shoulders. Everything depended on her. If she didn't come up with a good idea then the holiday really was going to be a disaster. She hadn't given up the chance of her first independent adventure away from her parents just to be stuck fending off lover-boy Steven with his bad breath and bulging frog eyes. No way!

"Do you think he'll be as disgusting as he was last year?" Kathy asked as she pulled the T shirt over her head?

"I sincerely hope not," said Susan. "Maybe he's had his braces off and stopped eating raw onions. That would be a big help. Remember when you gave him some bubble gum and it got stuck in his braces and he spent all morning trying to pick it out with his fingers?"

"I hope he doesn't come close to me and breath all over me," Kathy said, screwing up her nose. "Maybe I should get Mum's lavender scented cologne ready to spray at him."

"That would be a waste of perfume, Kiff. Remember the time he gave you those pretty windmills and made you that spectacular sand castle and wrote "I love you" with shells?"

"It wasn't spectacular," Kathy protested. "It fell over and anyway the windmills were Peter's. The only thing *I* remember is that he wouldn't leave me alone, not ever. He gave me those beautiful red roses and it turned out that he had taken them from the reception desk and dripped water all over the register. Trust Mrs. Gerty to see me stuffing them in the bin. He got us into real trouble over that. And the time he stepped in dog pooh and got it all over the carpet outside our hotel room door when he was putting the stinky love letter under the door."

"I know, Kathy," Susan answered her. "You don't have to remind me. I'm as desperate as you are to get rid of him."

The door burst open and Peter charged in the way he did when he was pretending to ride his stallion, Geronimo. "Yipee!" he shouted. "He'th here all right. He wathn't wearing his red thweater though. Thith year itth green."

"What about braces?"

"I dunno, thtupid. He had hith mouth clothed!"

Dad sat up in bed, bleary eyed and attempted to swing his heavy legs over the side of the bed.

"You three," he said, squinting at his watch and yawning. "Don't you know that it's only seven-thirty in the morning. Breakfast isn't until eight-thirty. I suggest that you get back into bed and read a book. You did all bring one, I imagine?"

"Can we go to the playroom instead?" Susan said. "Nanny always used to get there about seven o'clock."

"Just make sure you go down quietly," he said, giving them a no nonsense look. "I could do without any more complaints from Mrs. Gerty. Do you understand what I am saying?"

"Yes, Dad," the girls said in unison, hurrying to get dressed, after which, looking left and right they edged themselves out into the corridor, Peter going ahead of them to protect them from the enemy. They tiptoed down the stairs, across the deserted reception hall, past the dining room where waitresses were busy laying the tables, and quietly in through the playroom door. Closing it behind them they straightened their backs, breathed a sigh of relief and looked up to find themselves staring into the murky brown eyes of a chuckling Steven!

9

Romance is in the Air

"Hi gorgeous!" he said to Kathy. "Dad said he saw you in the corridor. Super that we're all here at the same time again, eh? Do you wanna come up to the room later to see the new laptop Mum bought me? It's got a fantastic graphic card and a really super fast processor. I've brought loads of DVDs with me, too, so I don't have to go down to the boring TV room this year. You can come and watch something if you like."

"Steven, we would just love to stay and chat," Susan interrupted him, "but we have to go to the dining room to ask the cook if they have rye bread instead of white. You know – for Peter's allergies!"

"I'll come with you if you like," said Steven.

Since there was nothing they could do to prevent him from joining them, Susan chose another tactic. Grabbing Kathy's arm, she said, "Hey, boys you go on ahead and we'll catch up with you in a minute. I've just remembered Mum asked us to ask Nanny about this evening." And with that Susan ushered her bemused sister back in to the playroom.

"You fibber! Mum didn't..."

"I know she didn't. And before you say anything about rye bread - of course, Peter doesn't have allergies but I had to think of something quickly. Sometimes telling a white lie is necessary."

"Why is it called a white lie?" Kathy asked innocently.

"I don't know. It just is."

In the meantime, the boys were having a man to man talk. "Hey, nipper," Steven said, "has your sister got a boyfriend?"

"Yeth, a different one every month! Everyone like'th our Thuth." Peter felt really grown up when he spoke like Dad.

"No, not Susan, you dork. Kathy?"

"Kathy? No, of courth not. She's only eleven!"

"Do you think she'd like one?"

"What? A boyfriend? I dunno! I'll athk her if you like."

"No, it's all right. I'll ask her, if it's all the same with you." Both boys looked over their shoulders to see if the girls were following. They weren't.

There were only two girls in the playroom when Susan and Kathy returned and they were so engrossed in playing with their Barbie dolls that the sisters were free to chat with Nanny without any interruption.

"Well, my dears. Romance is in the air again, I see! Oh, I'm sorry. Have I said the wrong thing? I must say he's very sweet on you, that boy. Steven is it? Oh, yes, a sweet lad!"

"Nanny, how can you say that? He's absolutely disgusting." Even Susan was surprised to hear Kathy sound so vehement.

"There, there. He might have his quirks my dear. Which one of us doesn't? Anyway with his Mum being away so much it'll be nice for him to have some female company."

"Oh Nanny!" Kathy cried.

"We thought his parents were divorced or something," said Susan. "She wasn't here at all with Steven and his dad last year."

"Oh no, my loves. I've heard that she's a very beautiful lady. An actress or something. I've heard say that she's doing adverts but then I don't have much time for the telly so I wouldn't know. All I *do* know is she's a very busy young woman, but your young lad..."

"He's *NOT MY YOUNG LAD,*" Kathy announced.

"No? Well anyway. Where was I now? Oh yes. Steven tells me she's coming next week so you'll see for yourselves!"

Susan and Kathy looked at each other in disbelief. Steven with a pretty mother? With his crooked teeth, smelly breath, terrible taste in clothes and bogeys which got bigger and then deflated like little balloons when he was talking – it couldn't be true. His dad fitted perfectly in the family portrait with his long, greying, skinny rat's tail hanging down his back pretending to be a trendy pony tail, his baggy jumpers and clingingly-tight swimming trucks and yuk – his hairy legs. He was an artist apparently. Yes, he fit! But a stunning mother? NO WAY!

When Nanny's attention was drawn away by the two little girls swiping at each other with their dolls Susan and Kathy made their exit. When they were outside Kathy held onto Susan tightly. "Remember saying that we would play a prank on Gerty?" she said. "Well, first help me to find a way of getting rid of Steve. *Please!*"

But in the end, Susan didn't have to do a thing because, directly after breakfast, the problem was solved for them.

10

The Top Landing

There were some traditions in the Thomas family that always had to be preserved such as beef and chips on Christmas Eve. The *Thomas traditional Teignmouth breakfast* was another. It was as the children were enjoying the unusual combination of a bowlful of prunes followed by sardines on toast that Steven walked casually over to their table.

"How about a game of Hide'n'Seek?" he said.

"Oh, that's a lovely idea." Mum said, oblivious of the fact that Kathy was cowering behind Susan and shaking her head. "You can all get down if you've finished."

"Thanks Mum," Susan said. "Come on you two."

"What did you say 'yes' for, you moron?" Kathy hissed.

"I know what I'm doing," Susan told her. "Trust me!"

"You'd better know what you are doing. I don't want to spend our first day with this blinking idiot!"

"Give us ten minutes Steven," Susan said calmly. "We'll meet you in Reception. I've just got to go to the room to get something."

"Super! See you in ten minutes." And with a gleam in his eyes and a breakfasty smile Steven turned back to his dad who was busy trying to swat a fly that was determined to land on his marmalade.

Ten minutes later saw everyone in Reception.

"Who'th counting first," asked Peter eager to start the game.

"I will," Steven announced eagerly.

"Kathy, let's go. Peter, coming?" Susan, Kathy and Peter charged across the hall so fast that Mrs. Gerty, who was registering a new guest, wasn't able to stop them although she did fix them with a glare which told Susan, at least, that the lady meant to deal with them later.

"Right, where are you both going to hide?" Susan asked.

"I'm going in the dollth' houth in the play room," said Peter.

"I want to come with *you,* Susan," said Kathy nervously.

"Oh, all right – if you must. Let's go up to the top landing. He'll never find us there."

"Can I come too?" asked Peter.

"Oh, Gordon Bennett! What about the dolls' house? Oh, all right, I suppose so. I guess we can all go together, but we'd better be quick."

Susan had been desperate to go to the top landing by herself. Over the previous two years it had become her favourite place to escape from the rest of the family so the idea of her sister and brother's accompanying her did not thrill her. But needs must.

Leading the way past their bedroom and up to the next floor, Susan turned left on the landing, and half running, half walking to the end of the corridor, stopped in front of a narrow door. Looking over her shoulder to make sure no one was watching she opened it, ushered Kathy and Peter inside and, glancing behind her one more time, shut it quickly. In front of them was a set of steep narrow stairs which twisted to the left at the top. If they met anyone coming down there was no way they would be able to get past.

"Thuthan, where are we going?" Peter demanded, breaking the silence. "Are we allowed up here?"

"It doesn't say we can't come up here, if that's what you are asking," Susan told him.

Kathy did not say a word.

Panting, they found themselves in front of a second narrow door which swung open as Susan nudged it with her finger. And there, in plain sight was the top landing, Susan's secret place. And although Kathy and Peter stared, Susan could see that they were disappointed.

11

Plans to Get Rid of Steven

Susan pulled a pretty little notebook and pencil from her back pocket.

"What'th that for?" Peter asked.

"I thought we'd write down some ideas of how to get rid of Steven," said Susan, opening the notebook to the first page and handing it to Kathy.

"What if someone sees us through the window?"

"Have you actually looked out of the window, Kathy? It's the back of the hotel. No one's going to be looking up here." As to prove her point, Susan went over to the window. regretting it as she did so since they were much higher than she remembered from the previous year. "Why don't we sit down now you've seen out."

"Look Thuthan, there'th our car! said Peter excitedly.

"Peter, come away from the window." Susan caught hold of Kathy's hand, her fear of heights turning her knees to jelly. She always felt better when she could feel someone close and the three sat down.

"Right - number one. Anyone got any ideas?"

"Thoot him!" suggested Peter.

"Don't be silly," said Kathy "why don't we just tell him to go away?"

"We tried that last year, Kathy and it didn't work a bit," Susan reminded her. "He even had to help us make our sand boat, remember?"

"Yeh, and he spent the whole morning boasting about how fantastic he is at cricket. I bet he can't even hold a bat!"

"That's it, Kathy. You've got it! We'll ask him to play cricket with us and put him on the sea side. He doesn't like water, remember! I can hit it over his head and make sure he has to keep running into the sea to get it back. Right. Now what about number two just in case he doesn't want to play cricket?"

"I could dare him to swim with me," said Kathy.

"But you thaid he'th thcared of water!"

"I know, Peter. He is! That's the whole point! He'll have to cross his heart and hope to die that, if he doesn't do what I dare him to, he'll leave us alone for the whole holiday!"

"He'll have to say he'll cut hith eye out ath well!" added Peter helpfully.

"Why?" Kathy asked, clearly confused.

"I think Peter is thinking of "poke a finger in my eye", Susan explained. "We can always try it and see what happens." Kathy jotted the idea down.

"Thuthan?"

"Yes, Peter."

"I need the loo!"

"You've got to be kidding?"

"No, I'm burthting!"

"Oh, for goodness sake!"

"It'th not my fault – it'th jutht pushing out."

"We don't need all the details, thank you! Kathy, will you take him downstairs to the bathroom?"

"What if Steven sees us? You come too, just in case. You always know what to say... please?"

"You two are useless! But I guess we've got enough ideas to be getting on with. Just promise me one thing, Kathy. Don't hang on to me like a three year old and please, try to smile at Steven when you ask him if he wants to swim with you!" Susan pocketed the notebook and they got to their feet. Peter went straight over to the window.

"Look, Dad'th looking in the car," Peter said. "I wonder if he'th trying to find uth?" And then, hopping from one foot to another, "Oh-oh I've got to go, guyth"

Susan, absorbed in something she had not noticed earlier, scarcely heard him. The window at the end of the landing, just a few meters away, was completely frosted over. Just like the window in the playroom.

12

Behind The Wall

"Kathy, you go down with Peter and I'll try to get Dad's attention," Susan said.

And then, as soon as Kathy had made a reluctant departure in Peter's wake, she got down on her knees and edged her way along the wall until she was opposite the window where, although she felt queasy, she stood up and rubbed the mist away.

What she saw disappointed her. The view was the same as it had been. Dad, with the door on the passenger side open, was clearly searching for something. And the steam. Well, it was coming out of the kitchen door which was propped open with an old wooden seat. But wait a minute. Something wasn't right. She hadn't had much time to see what was beyond the wall earlier but she was sure there had been nothing more than a piece of wasteland and lots of rubbish piled high there, but now - now there was an exclusive bungalow surrounded by large palm trees and colourful flower beds and, in the garden, a beautiful swimming pool! It couldn't be. She would have noticed that for sure. And so would Kathy and Peter.

Next to the pool was an old woman, sitting at a small round table, reading something. And coming out of the French windows onto the terrace was a boy not much older than herself. He was tall, blond and very handsome with a super sun tan! He walked over to the old lady, placed a tall glass on the table and stood looking down at her as she put her book down, took off her glasses and looked up at him, smiling fondly. And when he leaned over to kiss her cheek, the old woman took his face in her hands and kissed him on his forehead.

Susan was in love! Oh, she'd been in love before – many times. But this was different.

The woman gave the boy something and he walked round the pool, through the gate in the wall and past Susan's dad, who was just putting the key in the car door.

"Hey, Dad!" Susan wanted to cry out. "Stop him! Say something to him! Keep him there till I get down!" But her father apparently couldn't hear her because he didn't look up. Instead, he straightened up, put his keys in his pocket and walked back to the hotel – just behind Susan's new love.

That was enough for Susan. Top landing or no top landing, if she raced she might reach the reception hall in time to see him. It was not until she was flying down the stairs that she remembered she was wearing a pair of old, baggy trousers. Still, it was more important to see him than to worry about whether or not he would notice her.

And so Susan raced out of the door at the bottom of the stairs, along the corridor, down the wide flight of stairs and into the reception. But Mrs. Gerty was not going to be bypassed this time.

"YOU AGAIN?" she cried. "I WOULD HAVE THOUGHT YOUR PARENTS WOULD HAVE SPOKEN TO YOU. DON'T YOU EVER LEARN? YOU'RE COMING WITH ME YOUNG LADY!"

Susan was puffing and panting and only half listening to the old woman, intent on desperately trying to catch a glimpse of her handsome stranger. But even though she was able to see the main door over Mrs. Gerty's shoulder, he was nowhere in sight unlike her father who walked in through the door just in time to see the receptionist grabbing his daughter by the ear.

"That won't be necessary, Mrs. Gerty," he said. "I will take over from here. I take it that Susan has not been tiptoeing about again."

"YOU ARE ABSOLUTELY RIGHT." Mrs. Gerty did not bother to lower her voice. "SHE HAS NOT. MR. THOMAS, I THOUGHT I MADE MYSELF PERFECTLY CLEAR! I WILL NOT TOLERATE THIS SORT OF BEHAVIOUR ANY LONGER. I REALLY WILL NOT. I AM GOING TO HAVE TO SPEAK TO THE PROPRIETOR."

"I am so very sorry, Mrs. Gerty. You may be assured that it will not happen again. Will it, Susan!"

"No, Dad. I'm sorry Mrs. Gerty. May I go now?"

Susan was gutted. No way she'd see him now. But just in case, she walked out onto the steps and looked left and right. He was nowhere to be seen. Going back into the hotel she waited until her dad had finished speaking to Mrs. Gerty.

"Dad, you know that boy who walked past you in the car park? Which way did he go?"

"Which boy, Susan? There wasn't anyone in the car park as far as I can recall and in fact, I remember thinking how quiet it was and wondering if our car was safe."

"But there was a boy, I saw him."

"I think Mum is almost ready to go over to the beach," he said, shrugging. "Go and get your things ready."

Susan knew that she could not let something as important as this just be dropped. "Can I have the car keys," she said. "I left my sunhat on the back seat."

Susan was excited as she hurried around to the back of the hotel. She had been sure that the wall was hiding something and now she knew what! Wow! This was going to be a holiday to beat all holidays! Passing the kitchen door she made straight for the wall, but although she looked and looked again, there was *no* door.

What's going on? First the misty windows in the playroom and on the top landing. What was wrong with her? She knew she had a good imagination but this was ridiculous. Neither picture made any sense, but both of them were so real. There had to be a door there. But try as she might Susan could not find the door that she had seen so clearly from the landing window. Looking up she was even able to see that window, the fourth from the right. She had seen the boy from it. And the old lady. And the pool. It had to be there. She just wasn't looking in the right place.

Spinning round on her heels, Susan made her way back into the hotel, this time being careful to *walk* past Mrs. Gerty. She made it to the top landing without bumping into anyone, and almost unaware of the height, she looked out of the window. What she saw made her hopes plummet. There, behind the wall, just beyond Dad's car was a desolate piece of wasteland. Piles of earth in one corner and an old sofa leaning up against what looked like an old barrack. No house, no patio, no table, no swimming pool, no old lady and – no door in the wall.

Suddenly Susan became aware of how high up she was and she felt her knees crumple. But even though she felt safer when the door to the landing was shut behind her, she was overcome by a sense of hopelessness. What had happened to what she had seen?

It just didn't make sense.

13

Dad Helps Out

"Susan! Susan!"

Voices from the corridor below forced Susan back to reality. She did not want them to discover her secret hideaway and had to prevent the possibility that Kathy and Peter might lead them there. As the voices became fainter, Susan made her way downstairs and, opening it slightly, was relieved to see an empty corridor. She was standing with her hand on the door knob to her room when Mum came round the corner.

"Where were you?" she fussed. "We've been worried sick. Dad said you'd gone to the car but there was no sign of you anywhere. We checked all over the hotel."

"I'm sorry, I er... couldn't find my sunhat and then..."

"Oh, there you are," said Dad, obviously relieved. Susan saw him throw a glance at Mum and, having expected a barrage of questions, was surprised when he fell silent.

"Where are Kathy and Peter?" Susan asked.

"Playing in the games room, with that Steven boy," said Mum.

"Oh, no!" Susan dreaded seeing Kathy. She would never forgive her.

"Get your things, Susan," said Dad holding the door open for her. "Mary, why don't you go and get the other two and go on down to the beach. Susan and I will catch up."

So she was to be left alone with Dad! Susan's worst fear was about to be realized.

"Finally, a moment alone, Suz," he said, when the others had gone. "How's my big girl?"

"Everything's fine, Dad."

"Happy to be back?"

"Yes, I'm happy." But she knew she didn't sound terribly convincing. Dad didn't say anything but when he gave her a hug she knew that he knew something was not right. If only she could tell him, she thought. But tell him what? The moment passed, although, as they left the hotel, she caught him looking at her curiously. They walked down to the beach together and found Peter, Kathy and Mum with towels spread out neatly and windshield in place. Kathy and Peter were jumping over the waves. With Steven!

"Has that boy been bothering Kathy?" Dad asked Mum.

"Well, he certainly seems a very lonely lad. I haven't seen his mother around at all."

"She's not coming until next week," Susan told them. "She's doing a film or something. Nanny says she's very beautiful."

"You seem to know rather a lot, young lady," Dad told her. "Mary, I think we need to keep our eye on him, and Kathy. The last thing we need is our daughter falling in love!"

"Fall in love with Steven!" Susan exclaimed, feeling herself blushing. "Dad, he's disgusting and he won't leave us alone."

"I think we might be able to help you with that. KATHY!"

Kathy turned and stared at him with what the family called a "Kathy stare," the kind of annoyed expression that had once caused a boy to fall off a wall.

"Yes, Dad," she said, coming to stand right in front of him. "What is it?"

"I think it's time for a boat building competition, don't you?"

"Competition? Why? We usually make one all together."

"Well, I was just thinking that you might like a bit of a break from your admirer's attentions."

Kathy's glare slowly changed into a smile.

"Oh, yes please," she said.

Susan was amazed. Who would have thought that Dad would come to their rescue like this?

"Wait right here," Dad said and returned a few minutes later with Peter and Steven on either side of him.

"Right then," he said. "Ready everybody? The idea is simple. Tunky, you and the girls against me and the boys. The best boat wins ice-creams."

The idea was a good one, all except for one thing. Dad was the boat-maker, not Mum. Right from the start the girls knew that they didn't stand a chance. But there was no time to worry. They just had to try and remember how Dad did it. Mum was no help. She'd never made one but she tried her best to dig with her fingertips for a few minutes, after which she sat on her towel and coached them from a distance.

"Don't do the seats first," Susan said. "We've got to get the outline done first. Look. Do it like this!"

Susan, having changed into her shorts while Dad was down at the water's edge, was down on all fours marking out the shape.

Then came the hard part. They had to dig and pile the sand up to make two raised seats and a raised front.

"This is impossible," she cried. "The sand won't stick! Look it's collapsing again."

"Girls, you've got your buckets," Dad called. "Why don't you go and get some water?"

"Of course," Susan said. "We are wallies. Mum, are you coming?"

But Mum, clearly not about to be lured into active participation again, told them that she would just keep an eye on the boat for them, and Susan was faced with the fact that if the contest was up to her and Kathy they'd better put a move on.

14

Bucket Chomping Harry

"You and Dad were such a long time getting here," Kathy complained as they raced to the water. "Steven found us as we were coming down the stairs."

"I'm really sorry, Kiff. I lost track of time and something happened. Oh blast! I've chosen the stupid bucket with holes in it."

Sure enough, Susan's bucket was already half full and emptying fast, water pouring down her sandy legs.

"It's okay. You build the boat, Susan, and I'll fetch the water. Ha, ha! Look at Steven!"

Steven was standing at the water's edge. The sleeves of his baggy jumper were rolled up above his elbows and he was trying to reach over as far as he could to fill his bucket without getting his toes wet, but each time he dipped the bucket in the wave it ran away from him almost as if it were teasing him.

"Scaredy cat, scaredy cat! Afraid of a little water!" Susan called out, but at once regretted it. His face, when he turned to look at her, was a ghastly shade of green.

"Gosh, Susan, look at him. He really *is* frightened of water!"

"I know, I've got eyes! I feel really stupid. But it's all right, Peter's coming to his rescue. Hey, Kathy, we're supposed to be building not gawping at Stevie boy. He'll think we're keen on him or something."

The girls returned to their challenge, Kathy glancing up every now and then to see how the boys were getting on. Susan wondered whether her sister was still feeling sorry for Steven – gosh, just so long as feeling sorry for him didn't turn into a modern version of *Romeo and Juliet*. She could see it now "Budding athlete marries actress's son."

"Susan, you've gone and squashed the seat."

"Oh, Blimme!"

"I thought you said that was a bad word."

"It is," said Susan. "Gran told me it's short for 'God blind me'!"

"Really?"

"That's what she said, but you know Gran!"

"Girls, I hate to tell you but the tractor's coming in this direction," Mum said. Susan looked up.

"Dad! Watch out! Bucket-Chomping-Harry's coming!"

"How have you got on, girls?"

"We've almost finished but Susan went and stood on the seat and it's all messed up," said Kathy.

"Never mind," Dad said, coming over to inspect. "Get in and I'll take a quick photo. You've done a splendid job and without much help from Mum, I see!"

"It'th rubbith!" said Peter.

"No, it's not. It's super. Almost as good as ours!" said Steven. He was looking at Kathy when he spoke and she lowered her gaze, her cheeks getting steadily pinker.

"Quick! Get in boys! Girls in the front!"

"I can't thee. Thuthan'th too big!"

"Stop fussing, Peter," said Susan patiently. "It's okay, Dad. I'll go behind."

"There's a girl. Right everyone. 1 – 2 – 3 Cheese!"

"Darly, I think you'd better hurry." Mum said as the tractor bore down on them, only to stop a scant five meters away. Out climbed a man in green overalls and a straw hat.

"Saw you building there, I did," said the driver, a cheerful, burly man with a long piece of straw dangling from his mouth. "Thought to meself – I can't go bulldozing children's masterpieces so I've just come over to have a peek. There now. My, that's um..! What is it?" It was easy to see why he had asked Susan realized, looking down. In their rush to get out of the tractor's way, they had rather messed their creation up.

"We made one ath well, Mithter- you wanna thee ourth?"

"Yes, please, my lad. Lead on!" Peter took him over to their boat and the man looked genuinely impressed. "I wish my granddaughter Anna could see this. Mind if I bring her down t' beach later to have a look? Though she's a bit shy is my Anna."

"Of course, you can Mr...?"

"Mr Blake - Harold Blake, though most people just call me 'Arry."

The children looked at each other in amazement. What a coincidence, Susan thought. Mr. 'Arry drives Bucket Chomping Harry!

"Well, I'd better be off." With a tip of his hat to Mum, he turned and was out of sight before anyone could say "Bob's your Uncle".

"What a lovely man!" Mum observed.

"I think it's time for those ice creams," Dad announced. "We'll call it a tie. Who's coming to the pier with me?"

"Me!" With the exception of Steven, all the children had jumped at the suggestion.

"Darly, it's almost lunch time. Shouldn't you wait till the afternoon. We don't want to spoil the children's appetites?"

"*Oh, Mum?*" the children groaned.

"I think they'll cope," Dad told her. "You will, won't you kids? After all, holidays only come round once a year and I fancy a bar of mint cream myself! Shall we get you something?"

"Well, if you insist," Mum replied. " I wouldn't say no to a vanilla sandwich myself."

While the family debated the matter, Steven stood a few meters away, tugging at his sleeves and burying his toes, nervously, into the sand. Susan knew it would be nice of them to ask him if he'd like an ice cream too, but if she offered once maybe he would want one every time and this was supposed to be a family holiday. She felt mean not saying anything and even meaner when she heard her Mum suggesting to Dad that he ask Steven to go with them.

"Darly, he's all alone on the beach. I'm sure his father won't mind."

"If you say so. But I am not sure what the girls will say."

"It's okay. He can come," said Kathy, who had sidled up to Dad while he was talking.

"What are you doing? I thought you wanted me to help you get rid of him and here you are inviting him along for ice cream," Susan asked Kathy as they followed the others down the promenade towards the pier.

"I don't know – it's sort of, well, I felt so sad for him when he couldn't go in the water. He's at a beach and he's afraid of water and his Mum's not here and he's all alone and - I just felt sad, that's all." Susan knew she felt the same way deep down inside and that this had been the right thing to do, and yet somehow, it just wasn't the same with someone tagging on.

"Just don't invite him every day!" Susan cautioned. "If you do, he'll expect to go everywhere with us."

"It's all right, sis. He wouldn't fit in our car anyway. That's it!" Kathy exclaimed. "We'll have to make sure we go places by car!"

Susan sighed. She was relieved. Even *she* could cope with Steven once.

15

The Pier

"Four Vanilla Twists, please," Dad said. "And... Sorry, Susan? Better make that three flakes, one orange lolly and one Vanilla Sandwich."

"That'll be four pound fifty, please, Sir," the ice cream lady said.

"I'm just going into the newsagents for a mint cream," Dad said, handing them their cones. "Don't run away!"

"The ice creams are more likely to run away than we are!" said Susan, having trouble opening the sticky wrapper of her orange lolly. How she wished he wouldn't treat her like a little girl.

"No mint creams, Dad?" she asked, when he returned, holding an enormous red bar of chocolate.

"Afraid not, but this'll keep me busy for a while!"

Susan, desperate to be on her own finally, decided now was a good a moment as any to suggest that Dad take the others back to Mum. "Dad, may I stay for a bit and have a look at the Whimsies?"

"Of course, you can, Suz. It's about time you had a few independent moments! You know where we are when you finish. Come on you lot. Susan will catch up with us."

Susan watched them walk off licking their cones. Peter had already managed to bite off the bottom of his cone and vanilla ice cream was beginning to squeeze out and trickle down his hand. Susan listened to the familiar fading admonishments of, "Quick, Pete, lick it" and, "Don't wipe your hand on your T shirt" while concentrating on finishing her own ice lolly before the sun finished it for her.

As she watched the tourists walk by, Susan's attention was caught by a boy who was helping an older woman hobble up the steps from the beach. Turning onto the promenade, they went into the souvenir shop just inches away from her to the left of the pier's main entrance. "It can't be? It is. It's him.... it's the boy through the window. And that old lady."

Susan flung what remained of her lolly in the wastebasket next to her, completely forgetting to read the joke that was written on the stick, jumped to her feet, determined to follow them, in the process of which she bumped right into a little boy holding a balloon, knocking him over and sending the balloon sailing over the side of the pier, higher and higher.

"I'm so sorry," she gasped. "I wasn't looking where I was going," she said as the little boy stared at her, wide eyed.

"That's all right," said the boy's mum, a rather elegantly dressed young lady. "It's the third balloon he's lost this morning, isn't it Johnny!"

The boy got to his feet, rubbing his knee and then, apparently realizing he had an audience, broke into a wail.

"There are not going to be any tantrums here, my boy," his mother said sternly. "And your knee is not bleeding. It was just a little bump. Don't look so upset," she told Susan. "He'll get over it. Now I mean it, Johnny!"

And just like that, the little boy went silent.

Susan was upset, all right, but not because of the balloon, but rather because, in all the furore, she had lost sight of her mystery boy who had disappeared again.

Colourful paper windmills spun gently in the breeze outside the pier, and sticks of rock and candy floss were temptingly displayed in little stands decorated with pictures of the pier and the light house. An inflatable dinghy and big blue rubber dolphin all but blocked the narrow entrance and as she squeezed past she found herself standing in a narrow gap between shelves packed to overflowing with plastic pink and orange buckets and spades, big green, floppy sun hats and shells stuck together cleverly to look like swans and elephants.

Normally Susan would have picked up item after item, asking herself which ones would make cute gifts for Helena and Gemma back home. This time, however, she sidled down the aisle to the end of the first shelf.

And then she saw him! Taking one step backwards to hide herself behind a pile of plastic coated place mats, she accidentally nudged a glass ball with her elbow and just managed to catch it before it rolled off the shelf. Then, pretending to be interested in a long bendy pencil, she edged closer to the end of the row.

"I think I prefer this one here," she overheard the old woman saying, "the one with the picture of the promenade. Your Mom will like it. Is it fudge or toffee? Oh, Lee, what am I gonna do without you?"

"Oh, Nan, you'll be comin' over to us in the fall," the boy replied. "Heck that's only three months from now. You'll be fine! Honest, you will."

"I know, Lee. It was so good of your Mom to let you come on your own. Just be sure and tell her how much I app...."

The voices became muffled and Susan, glancing up from the pencil that she had been twisting round her fingers, not wanting to miss a word, manoeuvred herself so that she could hear what they were saying more clearly.

"Sure thing, Nan. When are you starting on the house?"

"Well, the plans have to be accepted by the neighbours first, and then I have to find builders I can trust and then, well, we'll see. Just you make sure you come back and visit when it's all done."

"I will if you have a swimming pool!"

"Oh, Lee. You rascal. I don't know about that. It would be terribly expensive and summers here aren't as warm as they are in California."

Susan was so desperate to see her misty boy that she moved cautiously to the other side of the row. What did she have to lose? If he was American, which he most definitely was if his accent was anything to go by, and he was due to leave soon she just *had* to see him. She didn't even like fudge but she picked a box up all the same. It had a cute photo of a kitten sitting on a fluffy pink cushion and "Greetings from Teignmouth" in swirly gold letters. She would buy it for Mum. She was just behind him, almost touching him and close enough to smell the freshness of his spotless, perfectly ironed, white T-shirt, and to notice that he was wearing brand new, expensive trainers and really trendy shorts. His hair was cut just a little longer than Dad would have been happy with but even she could tell it had been styled by someone who knew what they were doing.

When he grinned at her and said "Hi," Susan was disconcerted. What should she do now? Good grief! Up close he was even more gorgeous!

"Sorry," he said. "Am I in your way?"

"No, it's all right," Susan assured him, her heart in her mouth. "I was just looking."

"Yes, I thought you were!" he said with a twinkle in his eye.

"No. I mean I was looking at the fudge," she heard herself say. "It's for my mum. She really likes fudge."

Now what had made her say a thing like that? Susan fretted he would think she was a real idiot. But when he looked at her with those beautiful brown eyes, how could she possible know what to say. To her horror, she could feel her cheeks burning.

"Do you want any more fudge, Nan? We should be getting back home. You know what the doctor said about being out in the midday sun – even if it is only the British sun!"

"You're right, my dear boy," she replied in a tired voice. "Lead on."

And the boy, putting the change back in his pocket, looked at Susan and said, "Bye."

"Bye." How pathetic was that! Susan was cross with herself for being such a wimp. Normally she had no problem flirting with the boys. But this time all she'd been able to manage was "Just looking at the fudge! My mum likes fudge." What an idiot! And now he was gone – just like that – gone. So the picture through the window was real after all. Lee did exist and so did his Nan. She would have to go back to the top landing and check one more time.

"That's one pound, fifty." Susan heard the shop girl, aggressively chewing gum, say in the sort of loud voice usually reserved for the deaf. "What's the matter? Don't you speak English?"

"Sorry," Susan said. "How much did you say again?

Taking the two pound coin she'd been saving for her Whimsey out of her pocket, Susan paid for the fudge and, pocketing the fifty pence change, she walked, squinting back out into the sunshine holding a pretty paper bag with the logo of the pier printed on both sides. Just ahead of her Lee and his Nan were walking slowly, arm in arm, Nan leaning on Lee for support – towards the lighthouse, the opposite direction to the hotel. But why were they going there if they lived behind the hotel? He had distinctly said that it was time for them to go home. Susan was certain he had.

"Did you buy the sea horse Whimsey you wanted, Susan? Go on. Show us." Kathy said when Susan found them, peering into the bag. "Fudge! What did you buy fudge for? Where's your Whimsey?"

"It's a long story. Mum, do you like fudge?"

"Yes, I do as a matter of fact. That's very kind, Susan, very kind." Mum took the fudge and Susan saw her giving her dad a quizzical look. "Does anyone have the time? I left my watch in the hotel."

"It's ten past one, Mrs. Thomas."

"Thank you, Steven. Just enough time for us to get in, washed up and down for dinner."

Everyone helped pack up but no one bothered to wash the sand off their feet like everyone else on the beach. The bowl of water on the top step just by the hotel's main entrance had been the suggestion of the owner's wife. The water was changed regularly and all the clients were expected to use it before entering. So they did, Peter jumping in, sending a shower of sandy water in all directions.

"Woopth, thorry!" he said, grinning from ear to ear.

"Thanks a bundle, Peter," Susan said. "Now the rest of us only have a centimetre left!"

The rest of the family rinsed as well as they could and wiped their feet with their sandy towels before putting their shoes and socks on and going in for lunch.

Looking over her shoulder as she walked up the steps, Susan wondered where the boy was and whether she would ever see him again.

16

Where is Steven?

"Toad in the Hole and baked beanth.   Yummy thcrummy!"

Toady sat up and scratched his head.
"Why am I here, in this dish?" he said.

"Just eat up, there's a good boy," said Mum. "I wonder where Steven has got to," she went on, cutting up a piece of steak and adding a green bean and a carrot to keep it company on the fork before dabbing it gently in the rich gravy and popping it into her mouth, licking her lips just to show how delicious it clearly was.

Susan watched her mother enviously. Why couldn't she have steak? she wondered. Why was it that at thirteen she was still considered a child and not the adult that she often felt she was and that her parents regularly demanded she act like.   But no. Instead it was Toad in the Hole and baked beans – again! She loved Toad in the Hole. But then she loved steak, too, and just sometimes, it would be *so* nice to be offered the chance to choose.

And then there was this business with Steven. Why all this concern for him all of a sudden? His breath still smelled, his taste in clothes was still atrocious and his hair looked like someone had ripped the ends instead of cutting them with sharp scissors. Susan looked over at his table. Maybe her mum was right. It did seem strange that his dad should be there slouching over a notebook while slopping away at what looked like green seaweed. Ugh! He eats with his mouth open. Phuj, how repulsive!

When he had just wiped his nose and mouth with the sleeve of his gaudy yellow shirt, Susan had to look away, "So that was where Steven got his manners, or rather lack of manners, from. It was disgusting. She could just hear what her dad would say if he caught *her* smearing her top with saliva and Toad in the Hole. "Now, Susan," he'd say. "Do you think you could refrain from transferring your food remains from your face to your garment! We do have such things as soap and water, you know."

Each detail of her life seemed to be under the scrutiny of her parents. On the other hand, sometimes she felt like a specimen that her biology teacher, Mrs. Davies, might ask her to study under a microscope.

It was so much nicer ignoring the details, she thought, now who wants to know what's crawling around on your toothbrush when you put it in your mouth at bedtime? Then again, maybe some things such as all the food bits sticking in Steven's braces were definitely worth dealing with.

She was off again. Everyone else at her table had finished their meal and she still had a sausage in batter left staring up at her. She found herself wondering who had thought of calling it a Toad in a Hole?

"Do you want your latht thauthage, Thuthan?" Peter said.

"Peter, you don't have to put it all in at once!" said Mum as Peter swiped it from Susan's plate and stuffed it in his mouth.

How many times had they heard that before? Susan asked herself.

Walking back to their room, the question of where Steven was, became evident.

"WHAT DO YOU MEAN YOU'VE LOST IT?" they heard his father say. "YOU RETARD. WHAT WILL YOUR MOTHER SAY? SHE SPENT GOOD MONEY ON THAT AND YOU GO AND LOSE IT ON DAY ONE."

"Sorry, Dad," Steven's voice was shaking. "I really am. It was just we were making a sand..."

"I DON'T GIVE A SHIT WHAT YOU WERE MAKING. IT COULD HAVE BEEN A BLOODY ROCKET FOR ALL I CARE. GOD, WHAT A LOSER!"

The door opposite burst open and Steven's dad stormed out and strode off down the corridor without a word to the family standing there. Everyone exchanged glances and then Dad opened the door to their room for them and they walked in silently.

So that's why Mum and Dad were being so nice. They must have known. But how? Kathy had been nice to him. Peter had talked to him as if they were old buddies but she had laughed at him. And now this. Eventually Mum spoke.

"Darly, do you think you could go and check on the boy?"

"Somehow I don't think his father would take kindly to our interfering," he said hesitantly.

Susan was interested to see what he was going to say next. After all this was his job. He had eight hundred boys under him and this one needed someone to stick up for him. Finally, without a word, he left the room and went to number 11. At first he simply tapped but then, when no one answered he knocked more and more firmly.

"Steven, it's Mr. Thomas, Kathy's dad," they heard him say in a loud voice. "Can you hear me?"

A few seconds later, Dad returned, his hand on Steven's shoulder. No-one dared speak, but everyone knows that silence gets uncomfortable after a while and this was no exception.

"What did you lose, Steven? Maybe we could help you find it?" Susan's heart felt a little lighter after she asked the question. She really did want to try and make up for being so mean earlier.

It was only then that Steven lifted his head. His eyes were red and puffy and his cheeks were tear-stained. "My cell-phone. I lost my cell phone."

"But you had it by the boat," Peter told him. "I thaw you putting it in your pocket."

"I know, but it's not there now and I can't find it in my room and Dad...Dad..."

"It's OK, Steven. We know. We heard. Come and sit down over here," Mum said tapping the bed next to her. Suddenly Susan had an idea.

"Dad, can't we go to the beach and look. Shame you haven't got your cell phone with you, you could call his number and we might hear it ringing." Dad never took his phone with him on holiday, arguing that this was his time off and if anyone wanted him they could jolly well wait till he was home again.

"There's my girl. Good idea. Steven, can you remember the number?"

As Steven told his number Dad jotted it down on the back of the hotel brochure which was lying on the bedside table and then beckoned to Susan and Kathy to follow him. "Peter, you stay here with Steven and Mum," he added, not giving Peter a chance to debate the matter and, girls, I'll see you across the road and ring from reception. If you find the phone answer it.

However, when he returned a few minutes later, he did not look happy.

"Sorry, girls," he said. "The phone's switched off, I'm afraid."

They spent half an hour raking the sand with their fingers round the sand boats. It wasn't until they were just about to give up that Kathy stood up and called out. "Look. On the back seat of our boat, where Steven was sitting. There's something there."

Scooping up a handful of sand she brushed the object clean. Apart from sand jammed down the sides of each button, the phone looked unscathed but they wouldn't know if it was still working until Steven switched it on again.

Steven was not as relieved to see the phone as they had expected or hoped.

"Dad'll freak when he sees all that sand," he muttered. "He'll go bezerk."

"Would it help if I spoke to him?" Dad suggested.

"No, he even shouted at my teacher once and called her a bloody tart."

"Right then, there's nothing for it but to see if we can't clean it up and then you can show him yourself. Mary, why don't you go down to the dining room and see if there's any Toad in the Hole left. Steven must be hungry."

"Oh, I like Toad in the Hole," Steven said. "Mum always calls it Frog in a Bog!" he added wistfully. "She's nice, my Mum."

Shame she wasn't here now, Susan thought.

Mum returned with lunch and Steven was soon tucking in. When he returned to his room ten minutes later it was with the promise that he would meet them all down on the beach when he was ready.

And so the afternoon passed. Steven joined the Thomases in a quiet game of cricket with the children making sure not to let the ball go anywhere near the water. They were treated to another ice-cream, and when they went in for tea, their new friend just looked at them and said, "Thank you, guys!"

Mum and Dad did not go out for their customary evening walk that evening. Instead they got out their pack of *UNO* cards which travelled everywhere with them, and the children were treated to the sight of a speedy, feisty battle between "The Oldies," as they sometimes called their parents. When the children were asked to join them for a rather more sedate version of the same game, Kathy and Peter got caught up in the atmosphere of competition as Mum and Dad taught them moves which would ensure a winning hand.

Susan bowed out early on. She could not understand what all the fuss was about. It was just a game, after all. But even she had to admit to herself that it was a cunning way of getting her brother and sister's minds of what they had witnessed earlier. Shame it wasn't working for her too.

At first another night was spent restlessly, as Susan dreamt of sand and seagulls, all resounding with a torrent of angry words. But as she finally drifted into a deeper sleep she found herself face to face with her misty boy. He took her hands in his and pulled her closer –his lips touching hers. He gently, oh so gently, moved a wisp of her hair out of her eyes and kissed her forehead.

"Sleep tight, my Suz. I love you," she heard someone say.

And for a moment, she thought it was the boy's voice she was hearing instead of Dad's.

17

Rain, Rain, Go Away!

Steven smiled again at breakfast but then disappeared until tea time. Susan enjoyed the peacefulness of the day. Finally a whole day to herself on the beach, sunbathing, swimming when she fancied cooling off, reading the next chapter of *Watership Down* and glancing up every now and then to watch her brother and sister taking it in turn to bat and field in a rather more exciting game of cricket than the day before, the ball frequently landing among the gently lapping waves which sometimes required a race into the sea.

As her friend Gemma would have said. "Why spoil a beach with a sport when you can sunbathe?" and Susan was inclined to agree with her.

Steven asked if they would like to watch a film on his lap-top after tea but Mum and Dad were quick to point out to their offspring that holidays were a time for relaxing together and not vegetating in front of a screen, be it a computer or a television. So Steven left them in the dining room, head hung low and dragging his feet.

Evening entailed a leisurely evening stroll along the promenade with "tiddldee om pom poms" being the only way the children were allowed to join in when their romantic parents, hand in hand, began to sing what they referred to as "old time favourites."

And all the time, Susan felt as though Lee was with her, his fingers entwined with hers as they shared tender kisses. Once again, Susan awoke the next day wishing she were in her own bedroom at home where she wouldn't have to fear someone overhearing her talking in her sleep.

Because of all that had happened with Lee, plus the fact that he seemed to be her constant imaginary companion, Susan had not gone back to the upper landing, fearing, on top of everything else, that she might wake up and find that everything had been a figment of her imagination. But how would she be able to explain the fudge then though? No, he was as real as she was. She was determined to believe what she had seen.

No one had mentioned the incident with Steven, but when they saw him at breakfast the next morning, they could all see that his life was not a bed of roses. He had been crying again. But there was no chance to say anything to him. His father glared at him every time he raised his head to look in their direction and he quickly dropped his gaze.

It was supposed to be another lazy day on the beach, but as is so often the way with English summers, the weather had other ideas. Having shoved all the towels, suntan lotions and buckets haphazardly in their beach bag the Thomas family headed happily for the front door only to find that rain had set in. Not the real heavy rain that relieved gardeners of their chore of watering their flowers every evening but the nonsensical drizzle which affects everyone's mood.

Instead of the delights of getting browner and more attractive by the hour Susan knew what the alternatives would be even before her parents suggested them.

"Now, then, let's make the most of today," Mum said. "You've all got a good book and Susan, I'm sure you brought your pencils. How about sketching something. And of course, I am sure Nanny would be pleased to see you all if you wanted to go down to the play, - sorry, I mean games room."

Susan had been spot on. Her parents' love of a good book made a wet day an ideal holiday day! But she'd had enough books for a while.

"I want to go thwimming!"

"It's raining."

"That's OK. The thea ith wet tho it doethn't matter!"

"Peter, the answer is "No," said Dad, his book already open.

"We'll go when it clears up," reassured Mum.

"I'm going to the gameth room, then."

"Me, too," added Kathy. That left Susan no choice. She wasn't in need of an intense conversation on any of the topics she expected her parents might raise for the sake of conversation. Mr. Kramer was out of his cupboard. She had lost weight running the full distance in her cross country lessons and she was making more of an effort with Steven. So off to the games room it was. At least this year they had added a table tennis table and a computer by the window for their older guests. Of course, Susan, Kathy and Peter didn't have a clue how to use the computer but, since they had a table tennis table in their garage back home that was where they headed.

Susan though, had one more objective, but it would mean getting Nanny on her own.

18

Nanny Explains

Steven was sitting in the corner when they walked in, his lap-top on his knees. Perhaps because of that, he didn't appear to have noticed them coming in.

"Why does it have to rain?" said Kathy.

"Gosh, you sound as grumpy as I feel," said Susan. "I just hope it clears up, that's all I can say."

"Susan?"

Yes, Kathy?"

"Oh, it's nothing"

"Go on, what's the matter, Kiff?"

"Promise you won't say anything unkind?"

"Sure, what is it?"

"Well... I don't want to play that joke on Steven. It doesn't feel right somehow. I thought I'd ask him if he wants to play table tennis instead. What do you think?"

"You're probably right. It wouldn't be fair now that we know what his life really looks like. Go on. You can ask him to play."

"What are you going to do?"

"I'll see if Nanny's free. There's something I want to ask her."

"Susan?"

"Yes?"

"Will you come with me?"

"What? To ask Steven to play? No! You want to play – you ask! By the way, where's Peter?"

"He was over by the window – look – I think that's him!" As Susan searched in the direction Kathy was pointing in she saw an over-sized boy riding a tricycle with a kettle dragging along behind. He was having some trouble pedalling with his legs up under his chin and his elbows sticking out to the sides. As usual he was laughing, which is more than can be said for the toddler who was chasing him.

"Gimme, gimme!" the child was crying.

"I think we'll let Nanny sort this one out!" said Susan. "Hey, I've just had a thought. How about planning some tricks to play on Farty Gerty. You can ask Steven to help if you like."

"Are you sure you don't mind? You were the one who said you didn't want him hanging around all the time?"

"That's not fair, Kathy. You..."

"So, squabbling, are we girls?"

"Hello, Nanny! No, it was nothing really, was it, Kathy?"

"No, nothing. Okay, I'll ask him."

"Why don't you play table tennis first and then come and find me. Not that there is anywhere to hide in here!" Susan said, as she turned from her sister back to Nanny.

"It's a shame it's so wet outside," Nanny observed, smiling as Susan sat down beside her. "I'll be guessing you'd prefer not to be stuck inside. I'm sure it'll clear before afternoon though. It usually does by the coast, you know."

"Nanny?"

"Yes, sweetie. What can I do for you? *Rosey, leave George alone, please! No, Rosey. He doesn't want Lego down his jumper!* Oh, that terror! She's worse than all the boys put together. Good thing her twin brother is down with a cold otherwise there would be pandemonium in here. Sorry, Susan. What were you asking?"

"It's silly, really."

"Out with it, my lass. Something's been bothering you ever since you arrived, if I am not mistaken?"

"No, this is something different." Susan did not want to be reminded of the hand episode although that still haunted her. No, she was more eager to find out anything she could about the mystery boy.

"Do you know what used to be behind the wall in the car park?"

"What, Love? That dreary old stone wall? Now, let me see. I've been here going on thirty-three years. I recall that there were plans for the hotel to buy the land to make gardens for our visitors but old Mr. Briar, the first owner, decided that folks come here for the sand and sea, not to sit in a garden. I always said he had a point, though it would have been nice to have had my own little flower display. I always fancied my hand at growing hyacinths. They have such a beautiful scent and look lovely among the tulips."

"So, there wasn't ever a swimming pool?"

"My, my. Now that would be silly. Indeed it would! Fancy anyone wanting a pool when the sea is just the other side of the road and the lido is right next door! But, wait a moment. Come to think of it, there was some gossip a couple of months ago that a foreigner had decided to build there and the word pool was mentioned. But how would a girl like you have come across that snippet of information?"

"I thought I saw... oh, it's nothing. Nanny, do you think they really will shut the hotel this year?"

"Yes, my lovely. I'm afraid this is to be our last summer."

"But why?"

"For a young lady you've got a lot of questions! It's the times, isn't it? We just can't seem to keep up with them. *Daniel, come here. There. Can't have your trousers falling down!* No! People don't want to sit on cosy little beaches on the south coast in the drizzle and stay in outdated hotels with no modern conveniences, not when Australia and Spain are on offer. They say that seaside towns like Teignmouth and Salcombe just aren't fashionable any longer. More hotels are being converted into holiday flats and they're all so expensive that only the upper crust can afford to buy them – you know, surgeons and business people. Nice people in themselves, but I must say I prefer my Thomases. *Rosey!* I don't understand their thinking at all. I've seen kids come in here this week and spend two hours in front of the computer while their parents are talking what they call 'shop' on their mobile phones in the lobby."

"Somehow family holidays where families are actually together seems to be something of the past. Sad, really. No, they are converting us into exclusive flats, they are, and I've been offered one if I like. But it wouldn't be the same. No, I'm heading back to sleepy Buntingford, I am. I'll miss the sea, though, that I will. *Rosey, that's it madam. Put him down.* I'll be back with you in just a moment, Susan. I need to be sorting this child out."

And with that, Nanny waddled off to tend to Rosey.

So there had never been a swimming pool. But there might be in the future. So, what she'd seen through the window might actually be a glimpse into the future, including the door in the wall, which was too weird. But if the conversation she had overheard on the pier was any indication, it might be true, which meant that the hand picture might be real as well.

Susan was beginning to feel uneasy.

19

Up to Mischief

"BOO"

"Good grief, Kathy," Susan exclaimed. "What the heck are you doing? You scared the living daylights out of me."

"Sorry, Sis. Didn't mean to make you jump!"

"Oh, Hi Steven," said Susan, noticing Steven cowering behind her sister.

"Hello!"

"So, who won?"

"He's really good! I bet he could even beat you!"

"You mean he beat you, Kathy? I don't believe it!" Steven looked pleased with himself.

"It was 21-19," he murmured.

"Oh, gosh, you must be good, Steven. Unless, of course, Kathy let you win!"

"SUSAN!" When Susan saw Kathy's expression she realized she had not been wrong.

"So it's time to have some fun with Farty Gerty," she said, changing the subject before Steven caught on.

"Yes!" Kathy exclaimed. "And Steven's got a really good idea."

"Calm down, Kathy. Let's go and sit in the corner. I've got my note book so we can jot some things down." Susan pulled up three buckets that had had building blocks in them at the beginning of the day, and turned them upside down to make seats, albeit not very comfortable ones. Opening the notebook to page one Susan quickly flipped over to the back cover. She had completely forgotten that her "Steven pranks" were on the first page! Fortunately no one seemed to notice.

"What about Peter? We can't plan anything without him. He'll be really cross if we do."

"Do you know what, Kathy. I think we'll leave him where he is for the moment, in his own world." And he was. Surrounded as he was by small cars and clearly happy with his two new friends it would have been a shame to disturb him.

Before many minutes passed, ideas were flowing fast and furious.

"We put drawing pins on a teacher's chair once but it stuck in her bottom when she sat down and she gave us all extra homework to do," Steven said. "We should have used glue instead. That wouldn't have hurt!"

"Steven, we can't do anything that is going to hurt her or damage her clothes, okay?"

"Sure, Susan. You're the oldest."

"What about chocolate mousse on the chair in reception?" Kathy suggested. "Can you imagine her face if she sat in it! She would go mental! It would look like she's sat in ..."

"Yes, Kathy. I think we all know what it would look like! But it would make a real mess."

"She's got plastic cups on the reception desk and a bottle of water. We could cut the bottom out of a cup and when she pours water in it it'll go all over her."

"Wow, Steven!" Susan exclaimed. That's a better version of balancing a cup of water on the door. With that joke it's always somebody else who gets wet. I like it! What do you think, Kathy?"

"Yeh, it's great. But how will we cut the cup?"

"I can do that," said Steven. Dad uses the same cups when he is painting. We can use one of his."

"OK, Steven. That's your job. I've got an idea too. It's something we did to Granma. Remember Kathy?"

"You mean with the mouse?"

"Yep!"

"What did you do?" asked Steven.

"Simple. Mum has a small finger puppet mouse. She keeps it in her handbag for some strange reason. Well, one day we dangled it over the banisters on invisible thread as Granma was coming up the stairs. Only, she was carrying a cup of tea and I hadn't realized just how terrified she was of mice," Susan could remember every detail as if it had been the day before. "Well, the result was pretty drastic. The tea went all over the wall and I thought Granma was going to have a heart attack." Steven was grinning at Susan's animated story.

"I've got some fishing tackle," Steven offered. "Would that do?"

"What's fishing tackle?" asked Kathy.

"The line you use to catch a fish with. It's invisible!"

"Super. Just one problem though," Susan added. "No banisters."

"We could hide it under the reception desk when she's not there and stand behind the corner and pull it."

"Good idea, Kathy. Do you think one prank is enough?" asked Susan who was beginning to realize that if she wasn't careful things were going to get out of hand.

"Well, I thought of one more," said Kathy, "but I'll have to whisper it."

"What is it?"

"Well, you know she's got no bosoms?" Kathy whispered in her ear. "Could we stick a sticky label on her back saying 'I've lost my bosoms. Has anyone seen them?'"

Susan exploded, falling backwards off her bucket as she stuffed a fist in her own mouth to muffle her laughter. It wasn't just what Kathy had said that had amused her but the thought of the expression on people's faces.

"Do you want to let me in on the joke?" asked Steven looking embarrassed.

"Oh, Sorry Steven," Susan said. "It wasn't about you. Honest! Kathy do you want to tell him or shall I?"

"You, You!" Kathy had been red-faced, but when Susan repeated what she had said she turned deathly pale.

"What are you laughing at, Thuthan?"

"Oh no! Peter. I'm not going to say it again! Steven, you can tell him everything later on. Okay?"

"No problem!" Steven said clearly chuffed at being included again. "When are we going to start?"

"Good question," Susan replied. "Look it will be dinner time in one hour. Why don't you get the fishing line and plastic cup and we'll get the sticky paper. Dad's got loads of little pads in his brief case. Kathy, you can try and get the mouse and we'll meet here after dinner. Hopefully, it'll still be raining!" Susan couldn't believe her own ears. Wanting rain? Well, it might turn out to be a fun afternoon after all.

"What are you going to do?" Peter insisted, obviously dying to know what they had been up to.

"Steven will tell you everything as long as you promise not to tell Mum and Dad." Susan told him.

"Croth my heart and hope to die."

"Right, Steven. He's all yours."

As the boys walked off together, heads close as they discussed in secret, Kathy leaned over to Susan. "Thanks for letting Steven join in."

"It's nice to see him smiling," Susan answered. "Gosh! I hadn't thought. What if he gets in trouble with his dad?"

"Can't we say he didn't do anything?" asked Kathy, looking genuinely concerned.

"Let's hope we don't have to say anything, but, yes." Susan said. "If we get caught we'll take all the blame."

As Kathy stood up Susan stretched and glanced down at the scribbles in her notebook with a grin. She was in her element. If the pranks worked they'd have a lot of fun. But if they back-fired she could just imagine the consequences. She really hoped everything would go according to plan.

20

The Mouse and the Label

"Back already, girls?" Dad said. "Mum and I have been talking about taking you over to Shaldon this afternoon. Fancy it?"

"Oh, no Dad. It's fine, really. We're doing a table tennis competition in the games room and anyway, we can't go to Shaldon. It's still raining."

"There are other ways of getting there, you know. The ferry isn't the only means."

"Oh, Dad. It wouldn't be the same. We can only go to Shaldon by ferry. It's always the best part of the holiday." Susan was getting desperate. She glanced despairingly at Kathy.

"Yes, Dad. Susan's right. We're fine. Honest. Steven beat me 21-19 and I have to get him back after lunch. And then Susan has to try and beat him and..."

"It's all right, girls. You don't have to get so worked up. It was just a suggestion, wasn't it, Mary?"

"Yeth" said Mum speaking with a needle between her teeth.

"What are you doing, Mum?" asked Kathy.

"Oh, I thought I would have a go at this cross stitch. Would you mind holding this for a moment? I seem to have got in a bit of a tangle."

Kathy walked over to where Mum was sitting surrounded on all sides by embroidery silks and piles of papers, which was nothing unusual. Mum always had piles of papers around her. She looked happy and totally engrossed. "I went a bit wrong here, but I don't think anyone will notice, do you?" she said, holding up what looked like a bird on a stick. "It's a Red Cardinal," she said proudly.

"I believe you," said Susan to herself rather than to Mum. Dad peered over his book.

"Very nice, Tunky" and promptly disappeared again. Susan didn't understand what Kathy was trying to signal to her at that moment, her eyes were darting from the bed to Susan and back again. But she knew it must be significant.

With Dad's nose buried in his book and Mum absorbed with her sewing Susan sauntered over to the bed to see the mouse sitting on some blue embroidery silk.

"This is a nice colour." Susan said as she picked up the thread and the mouse at the same time, pocketing the one as she held up the other.

"That's for the flecks on his wings," her mother said. "Here! See?"

"Oh, yes. Very pretty." Susan winked at Kathy who let out a sigh of relief. "One down, two to go!" Susan whispered to her sister as they headed down for dinner.

They hadn't had a chance to get into Dad's briefcase, but there was still plenty of time.

Peter and Steven, who were sitting together at the family table when Susan and Kathy arrived, looked up and sadly shook their heads.

"No luck," Steven told the two girls. "Dad was in the room, so we couldn't get them. He said he's not feeling very well and isn't even coming down for dinner."

Mum and Dad had stopped to talk to a couple who had been at the hotel the year before which gave the children some time to discuss what to do next.

"We need a plastic cup, yeth?"

"Yes," said Susan.

"Well, Mitheth Gerty alwayth comth in for lunch when we're jutht finishing so we could get one from her dethk then."

"Good point, but when do we put it back?" Kathy asked.

"Don't worry, Kathy. There'll be a moment. We'll just be ready and waiting," Susan said, knowing that perfect preparation would be the key to success. "What about the fishing tackle though? That'll be more tricky."

"Mum's got masses of silks, Susan," Kathy said. "What about finding one the same colour as the floor."

"But they're too thick, Kathy. Farty Gerty would see it for sure."

"Susan, you don't know anything. You split them until they're really thin."

"Okay, clever clogs! How are we going to get it without Mum seeing?"

"You got the mouse. I'll get the thread!"

"Ssh! They're coming!"

"Hello, Steven," Mum said. "Isn't your dad coming for dinner today?"

"No, Mrs. Thomas," Steven said, all smiles. "He's not feeling very well." Whereupon Mum busied herself organising Steven's place to be transferred to their table. While it made it a bit of a squash, nobody complained.

When Mrs. Gerty, glaring and clearly unhappy about something, strode into the dining room, Peter went into action.

"Mum," he whined. "I need the loo!"

"But you haven't finished your dinner yet," she fussed. "Oh, all right you can go but come straight back."

"Thanks, Mum." Peter made a dash for the door and returned grinning from ear to ear.

But when Kathy asked for the key to the room Dad's eyebrows went up.

"Something going on we should know about?"

"No, Dad. I just wanted to get my sweater. It's a bit breezy."

"Here you are," Dad said, handing her the key. Kathy also came back to the table looking very pleased with herself.

"Where's your jumper?" Dad asked, when Kathy returned empty-handed.

"Um, I couldn't find it! But I'm not cold now. I think running up the stairs helped!"

"Kathy!"

"Yes, Dad?"

"No running!"

"Oh, yes, I forgot!"

Dinner dragged, pudding dragged. Trust it to be the day that the owner came bringing cream cakes for all the adults.

"How come grownups always eat cream cakes so slowly?" Steven asked Kathy.

"I don't know, Maybe they like seeing us dribble and drool."

"Mum, can I have a lick? Pleathe?"

"You most certainly cannot, Peter. You didn't eat all your peas."

"I don't like peath, Mum!"

"You should eat them like I do," said Kathy. "Just swallow them whole."

"You mean you don't chew them?" Susan asked.

"Phew! You actually chew them. Yuk! How can you. They are all squishy."

"Children, please!"

"Sorry, Dad!"

"Mum, can we, sorry – May we get down?"

"What's the magic word?

"Mum, I'm thirteen. Everyone knows it's not a magic word, just like everyone knows that Father Ch.."

"Susan!"

"Well, it isn't!"

"Well, without the word, the answer is easy – NO!"

"*PLEASE*!"

"That's better. Yes, you may all be excused." The children dashed for the games room but the door was locked.

"It's always locked during meal times," Steven explained.

"What about the TV room?"

"Two chances." They went down the dark corridor and found the TV room door open but when they walked in they realized it wasn't going to be any use to them. As always the room was dimly lit. It was just possible to make out that the chairs were still made of dark red leather though in worse shape than the previous year. There was the same musty smell and the same old television was set into the wall. Susan was beginning to understand what Nanny had meant when she said the hotel wasn't "moving with the times." Even their school had interactive touch computer screens on the walls of several classrooms.

From somewhere near the back of the room somebody coughed a "do-you-mind-you-are-disturbing-us" kind of cough and they heard a girl giggle.

"What were they doing in the dark?" Peter asked as they retreated to the corridor.

"Probably math's homework!" Susan told him, winking at Kathy. "Let's sit over here." Together they sat down in the bay window, overlooking the car park.

"Why don't we get everything out and see what we've got." Peter pulled the plastic cup from under his jumper.

"It's a bit squashed," Susan mused as she pushed out one of the collapsed sides and checked for splits. "But if we do this to it, it should be all right."

"I've brought Mum's scissors so we can cut the bottom," Kathy told her.

"Great thinking, Kathy. Hand them over. I'll do the cutting. I don't suppose you thought about the sticky paper while you were in the room?"

"What are sisters for!" Kathy held up a bundle of sticky yellow papers and flapped them under her sister's nose triumphantly.

"That's why you looked so pleased with yourself!"

"Yep, and I got the thread. I didn't know what colour so I brought six. You can choose."

While Kathy and Steven busied themselves dividing silks and tying one end round the mouse's neck, Susan cut the bottom neatly out of the cup and Peter tried to stick four labels together but made such a pig's ear of it that Susan had to take over, sending Peter, instead, to the kitchen to ask for a pen.

Eventually they were ready. Peter was given the task of look out and it wasn't long before he came racing back.

"She'th gone to the laundry room. Nobody'th at reception."

"Quick. Steven, you take the cup. I'll put the mouse under the desk. Kathy, you get the string and unwind it so that it goes round the corner."

"What thall I do?"

"Peter, you keep watch and tell us when she's coming!"

"Who's going to put the label on her back?" asked Kathy.

"I don't know yet!" Susan answered excitedly.

People were beginning to make their way back to their rooms after dinner but the children managed to get everything in place without being spotted.

"She'th coming," Peter hissed. "She'th coming"

"Right everyone. Round the corner. Quick!"

"The thread's knotted," said Kathy panicking as she tugged at the silk.

"Where?"

"Here!"

"Give it to me." Susan deftly loosened the knot and handed the end back to Kathy. Then they crouched quietly just out of sight round the corner behind the reception desk, every now and then peering out to see what was going on.

Mrs. Gerty lifted herself onto the tall swivel chair behind her desk and patted her lap. From the other side of the counter Paddy plodded lethargically towards her and tried to leap onto her knees. But he was too heavy, and after three failed attempts Mrs. Gerty, heaving a sigh, picked him up and plopped him unceremoniously on her lap and began the thankless task of registering newcomers.

The first to arrive was a man in a smart suit, drizzle lining his forehead. He put a briefcase on the desk, took out a handkerchief from his pocket and wiped his face, put the hanky back and nodded to Mrs. Gerty.

"Mr. Robinson here," he said. "I believe you registered my wife and twins two days ago."

"Ah, Yes, Mr. Robinson. I've put them in room fourteen. Here is the second set of keys. I'll just call the bell boy to take you up."

"That would be very kind of you, indeed. Thank you."

Mrs. Gerty pushed the buzzer and they waited in silence until the man said, "Shame about the weather. Has it been wet all week?"

"Oh no, Sir. Only since this morning. Would you like something to drink, Sir? I don't know what can have happened to the bell boy."

"Yes please. I see you have a bottle of water. If you have a cup, that would do very nicely. I have just walked from the station and it's further than the brochure indicated."

"*NO! NO! NO! Not that cup!*" *Oh, please, God. Not that cup!*"

The children held their breaths as Mrs. Gerty, having handed the cup to the gentleman, took the lid off the bottle and began to pour, whereupon the water, just as they had intended, went straight through the cup. But instead of going all over Farty Gerty it splashed and sloshed all over the man's briefcase before dribbling all over the desk and down onto the floor, so astonishing Mrs. Gerty that she jumped up dislodging poor Paddy who landed with a thud on the floor. Rolling himself slowly over, he sat up looking dazed and started licking his shoulder.

"Whoops!" whispered Steven.

"Right, it's my turn. Watch this!" As she spoke, Susan stood up and walked courageously round the corner.

"Oh, dear!" she exclaimed. "What happened? May I help, Mrs. Gerty?" Susan offered, taking the opportunity to press the label onto the old woman's back but making it look like a friendly pat.

"Oh, the Thomas girl," Mrs. Gerty exclaimed. "Run to the kitchen and get one of the waiters to bring a mop. Run, girl. Don't just stand there!"

"Run, Mrs. Gerty. Do you really want me to run?"

"Don't be impertinent, child. Simply do as I say."

"This should be fun!" Susan told the others, who were still lurking around the corner, before fetching the waiter who obediently wiped up the puddle while Mrs. Gerty hovered over him.

"I am so sorry, Mr. Robinson," she said. "I don't understand what could have happened."

"It looks like a manufacturer's fault to me," he told her, dabbing at his sleeve with his handkerchief. "Can't be helped. No-one's to blame. Ah, you must be the bell boy. Room fourteen, Please. Good day, Mrs. Gerty. Please don't worry yourself. Accidents happen."

Mrs. Gerty sat herself back down with considerable difficulty.

"Look at Paddy! He looks really offended."

Susan was right. Mrs. Gerty had left him on the floor. He was sitting with his back to her as if he was still cross at being tossed off without a stroke or an apology.

"When shall we do the mouse?" asked Kathy.

"Wait until Mrs. Gerty calms down a bit! said Susan. "Peter and Steven, do you want to go and see if the games room is open yet?"

"You've gotta be kidding. I'm not going to miss this!" Steven's eyes were bright.

"I'm thtaying if he'th thtaying," said Peter. And so they all waited while two more families arrived and were shown to their rooms.

"Right, now's our chance!" Susan said when Mrs. Gerty was alone again. "Ready, Kiff?"

"You do it, Susan!"

"Oh, Kathy, come on. It's your job. I put the label on her back."

"I'll do it," Steven offered. Susan and Kathy looked at each other. "Go on, you guys. Please!"

Reluctantly, Kathy handed him the end of the string. Kneeling down he took a peek. "Here goes," he whispered. "Oh blast, it's stuck. Here. Look. Now it's under one leg of her chair."

And although they all took turns pulling, there was no budging it until, as luck would have it, the next person who came to reception asked for some brochures of the town and Mrs. Gerty had to go over to a small wooden cupboard. As she moved the chair back, the thread was released and the mouse began to move. Slowly, very slowly. Mrs. Gerty had her back to the children's corner but Paddy was inches from the creature. Even asleep his ears came forward and, without seeming to move a muscle, his eyes opened and he was ready for the kill.

"Paddy'th theen the mouth!" Peter said excitedly.

"Pull, Steven. Now!" Susan whispered.

So Steven pulled. The mouse responded. Paddy pounced. And Mrs. Gerty, turning, screamed. A split second later, she was standing on her chair while Paddy, in hot pursuit of the mouse, followed it round the corner and skidded to a halt in front of the children who were giggling fit to burst.

"Quickly, hide the mouse in your pocket, Steven!" Susan said. "Kathy, you and Peter walk across the reception and straight up to the bedroom, Steven, you go to the games room and wait for us. Right, everyone. Go!"

Still giggling, Kathy and Peter walked slowly across the reception hall before speeding round the corner and up the stairs. Steven retreated, giggling, to the games room and Susan, stifling her laughter, waited a minute or two before following her brother and sister.

"Did you see a mouse?" Mrs. Gerty demanded.

"I don't know, Ma'am," Susan replied. "Your cat ran past me in the corridor but I didn't see if he was chasing anything." When there was no response, Susan calmly made her way across the lobby where, by now, a crowd had gathered, watching Mrs. Gerty prance about precariously on her chair, displaying, with every turn the card attached to her back which announced:

I have lost my bosoms.

Has anyone seen them?

Their next chore was to retrieve the sign before Mrs. Gerty discovered it and put two and two together.

In the end, it was Peter who came up with a plan. Paddy having disappeared, Mrs. Gerty was able to descend. The crowd eventually dispersed and Peter, who presumably had been watching everything from the safety of the stairs, sauntered back across the lobby, his hands in his pockets doing his best to whistle. In an Oscar winning performance, he managed to slip and lay writhing on the floor, groaning and holding his ankle until Mrs. Gerty, temporarily diverted from her panic attack, stooped down and ordered him to put his arm around her neck as she lifted him slowly to his feet. His cure was almost instantaneous.

"Oh, that'th better! Thank you Mitheth Gerty. I'm fine now."

"Be off with you," she growled.

Peter hobbled over to the girls.

"You dafty. You are limping on the wrong leg!" Susan said as she watched him hobble on ahead of her.

"You mean like thith?" he asked, promptly swapping legs.

"Stop it or she'll see you! Where's the label?"

"Here!" Peter handed Susan the crumpled mess of sticky yellow paper tags.

"I'd better get rid of this before Mum goes through my pockets. Now all we've got to do is get the mouse back in Mum's bag."

By tea time everything was back in its place, with Mum none the wiser. Perhaps because their friendship with Steven was sealed, it seemed to Susan that he was actually beginning to take more care of his appearance. At all events their drizzly day had been such a resounding success, all things considered that they topped their evening off with the table tennis tournament that they'd been promising themselves. Steven actually beat Kathy again *and* Peter, but was stumped when playing Susan who, at least in this sport, was a rival to be reckoned with.

21

The Ferry

"Wake up, Wake up, It'th thunny! It'th thunny!"

"Go away, Peter. I'm in the middle of a dream," Susan said, and she was.

In it, Lee had asked Susan out on a date and they had spent the most romantic of evenings wandering hand in hand along the promenade until they reached his favourite spot at the Shaldon end of the beach. There they had sat on the uneven, stony surface leaning against the wall and looking out across the water to Ness Head, the sun still shining warmly on the quaint, colourful houses on the Shaldon side of the water. It was an idyllic setting in which they sat contentedly, watching the seagulls swoop over the retreating tide. In fact, they had sat there so long that Susan had found that, when she tried to get up, the pins and needles in her leg made it necessary for Lee to help her to her feet. Arm in arm, they returned to the hotel, talking companionably.

Lee had just said he wanted to ask her something when Peter's cries had snatched him away from her.

"Rise and shine, lazy bones," she heard her Dad say. "Your sister was up and about an hour ago and even Mum is dressed." Susan looked up to see Dad in shorts she thought were just a little too small for him. Oh, well, at least here he didn't wear his slippers on the beach. At home he wore them everywhere – even to do the gardening.

"Mum up? No way! Oh Dad, can't I have another ten minutes?"

"I fear not. You'll miss your breakfast if you do, not to mention the ferry to Shaldon."

"Ferry to Shaldon?" Susan bolted upright against the pillows. "Really? Today?" She was up and dressed and eating breakfast with Mum in five minutes. There was no way she was going to miss the ferry to Shaldon.

"How's your father today, Steven?" Mum asked the boy when he came walking into the dining room, clearly looking for something.

"Not feeling well, Mrs. Thomas. He says he's got a hand over."

"A hand over, eh?" she told him, and Susan could see she was not amused. "Well, that would explain a lot. You're looking smart. Is your mum arriving today?"

"No, Mum isn't coming till Wednesday. But Kathy said she'd beat me at table tennis."

"I'm afraid we're going out for the day, Steven, but maybe she'll play you in the evening when she gets back."

Susan felt a pang as she saw the way he seemed to slump into himself. "Oh," he said, backing out of the door.

"Shame he can't come with us really," Mum said when he left the room, his head hanging low. "Kathy and he are starting to get on really well and Peter likes him too."

"What about you, Susan?" Dad asked.

Susan didn't know what to say. Ordinarily she'd be jealous sharing their family time alone together with anyone, but her thoughts were so full of her misty boy that it was as if she didn't have time or energy for negative thoughts. Finally she had something which wasn't under the scrutiny of her parents or her sister. Kathy had always known about her secrets and had even slipped out of the house with her on one occasion to meet a secret boyfriend – providing an excellent alibi when Mum asked where they'd been. But no one knew about Lee and she was determined that no one would find out.

"He's OK. Mum. He's nicer than last year."

"Maybe that's because you're all being nicer to him."

"Mum?"

"Yes, Susan?"

"Can we......"

"What? Go to Ness Cove?"

"Yes. How did you know I wanted to go to Ness?"

"Oh, Susan, if you could see the way your eyes light up even at the thought you'd know how I knew."

Susan was worried. She didn't know her eyes spoke. Crumbs! How was she going to keep Lee a secret if her Mum could read what she was thinking by looking at her eyes? Did this mean that she'd have to walk around with her eyes closed or try to be thinking about something sad whenever her parents looked at her. Life was so complicated!

"I don't know why we're sitting here talking when we could be on our way!" Mum said. And she was right. The others had long since gone up to the room to get ready. If yesterday had been a fun day then today would be pure magic. Susan could feel her eyes begin to sparkle.

As they got into the car, Susan noticed that Steven was standing, leaning against the railing of the promenade, opposite the hotel, hands in his pockets, shoulders sagging. She pretended not to see him because she didn't want to feel guilty or carry his loneliness with her throughout the day, but she did feel unhappy at the thought that he would be by himself again.

Kathy noticed him though and Kathy waved. "Mum," she cried, loud enough for him to hear. "Can't we invite Steven?"

"No, Kathy," Mum replied patiently. "We've only got room for five."

Steven waved, only to let his hand drop slowly to his side. Looking out of the back window Susan saw that he was still standing looking dejected as Dad pulled away from the hotel.

It was a glorious day and the seafront was bustling with happy holidaymakers. Children skipped joyfully along the promenade, couples strolled arm in arm, mums pushed strollers and dads took photographs of their happy families.

Passing the pier they saw a crowd gathered, and through Mum's open window there came the sound of jazz. Out in the bay they could just make out the RNLI lifeboat which would be on display all day, and Susan knew, from past years that the men who operated the boats would be there to tell about their daring rescues. There might even be a demonstration or two, with plastic sharks and men pretending to be in trouble, falling dramatically overboard to the delight of the onlookers.

It was, Susan knew, the perfect day for them to go to Ness Cove since, with most of the tourists heading for Teignmouth, the charming streets of Shaldon would be empty of holidaymakers, the tunnel even more mysterious and the Cove their own for the day.

Normally they walked through the town square, but Dad had chosen to bring the car today. Susan was sad. She would have liked to walk past St. Michael's into the Triangles and past the fountain. She might have been able to persuade her mum and dad to buy some liquorice in Sweet Memories and she could have asked Donna how she made the delicious hand-made, mouth-watering chocolates that were so beautifully decorated, and just out of reach, in the glass display case.

It would have been a lot of fun to stop the car and savour the excitement of the carnival, but on the other hand, Dad always said he had enough of screaming children during the school year.

Instead, they drove the whole length of the promenade, against the flow, streams of tourists walking in the opposite direction. Continuing right to the end they found a place to stop in the car park just above where she and Lee had sat in her dreams. They were just in time to avoid the procession which was beginning to form at the end of the crowded street.

It was quiet here. Magnificent Georgian hotels lined the streets and the peaceful waters of the river Teign lay just ahead of them. Small sailing boats dotted the water, their sails adding a splash of colour to an already picturesque scene and fishing boats wove their way cleverly between exclusive, moored yachts, out of the river into the open sea. With the picnic basket wedged safely under his arm, Dad led the way down onto the sand.

There, standing at the edge of the water, waves splashing gently on her bow, was the ferry, her plank fully extended and wedged safely in the sand. A man dressed in a thick, cuddly blue fleece and a white peaked cap, was helping an older gentleman to disembark. The ferry had clearly just arrived, bringing a group over from Shaldon.

The tide was out and there was quite a walk down to the ferry, first on warm sand which changed into pebbles the lower they got. Try as hard as they might, each footprint sank deeper than the previous one until, just a few meters from the boat, each indentation immediately filled with water as little rivulets trickled into them from puddles left from a higher tide.

They waited as the ferryman helped the final passenger off, a young man, whose attention was so focused on the conversation he was carrying on on his mobile that he literally slithered his way down to the beach. Then it was their turn. Mum held out her hand and was soon walking up, followed promptly by Kathy who help on tight to Dad's hand until his feet were dangerously close to the river. As for Peter, he ran up by himself ignoring the warning of the ferry man who called out, "Be careful, my lad. I had a boy about your age fall in once!"

Dad made way for Susan to go up next, but made no objection when she indicated that she wanted to stay put for a moment, savouring the occasion so intensely that she wasn't even aware that there were people standing behind her. At that moment it was as if she were all alone. She had watched the film *Titanic* at Gemma's house after their exams had finished and, walking up the plank, she felt, just for a moment, as if she was boarding a cruise liner, dressed in an elegant gown, a fur draped round her shoulders. She could even imagine, she found, that she was being escorted aboard by a young, handsome gentleman.

"Mind the step down, Miss,"

Those words brought her abruptly back to reality and she thanked him.

"You're very welcome, I'm sure!" said the ferryman, a gentle smile etched on his suntanned face. "Welcome aboard. Make yourself comfortable! It won't be long before we set sail."

Susan was embarrassed by the possibility that he was playing along with her fantasy. Could he, she wondered, sense her excitement, though why she should be quite so thrilled to be getting onto a small ferry with a black and white chequered side and little flags struggling to fly in the gentle breeze she would have found hard to explain - even to herself.

The ferryman released her hand and she looked up into his tanned, lined face. He was a kind man, she thought, with smiley eyes like Grampa, eyes which she would be happy to trust.

"Whoops!" she'd forgotten that sensation – the one that reminds you you're not on solid ground. The boat wobbled and then wobbled again, even more this time. The family seemed to be bothered by it more than usual. Peter, at least, was staring at something, mouth agape, and Kathy was looking just plain uncomfortable. As Susan found her place next to Dad, she looked up and saw the reason for her family's discomfort. Coming onto the ferry was the largest man she'd ever seen. She had once watched a Sumo-wrestler on TV but had quickly been advised by her Mum that it was, "not a suitable programme for a young lady." Well, this man would have won the Sumo- championships, because he was so huge. It was hard not to smile. But the realization that this person was going to be travelling with them across the Teign river in their little ferry was a worrying thought at best and so the smile didn't appear.

There was an awkward moment when the ferryman had to suggest that the man turn sideways as he got on board to be able to get between the barrier at the top of the plank, awkward because he was as wide sideways as he was when he was facing forwards. Susan knew she was staring but it was impossible to look the other way. She had to see how he would manage. He did! Just about.

The ferryman was as polite and jolly with him as he had been with Susan and ushered him to the seat next to Susan who took a deep breath!

"Don't worry! I promise I won't squash you," he said, smiling down at her, his cheeks and chin and neck all rolling into one.

Susan didn't reply. Not because she couldn't think of anything to say – Oh no! She could think of plenty of witty responses, but the man was already paying attention to the next person being brought on board, a petite Japanese woman with long straight black hair hanging in a pony tail, dressed in the most exquisite outfit Susan had ever laid eyes on. And she was delicate in everything she did, in the dainty way she held the ferryman's hand, touching it with just her finger tips, the tiny steps which made her appear to float up the plank and the graceful way she gathered up her kimono, if that was the right name for it, as she was seated, smiling shyly. For a moment Susan thought that, impossible as it seemed, they might be together, and then she really did feel as if she had been transported into another world or at least onto a film set at Hollywood.

With the ferry tilting to one side Susan felt relieved to see that there was only one more person waiting to get on the boat, a young woman who seemed to know the ferry man quite well, calling him Jim and then whispering something in his ear as he helped her to her seat.

Several years older than Susan, and much more beautiful, the girl was dressed in tight jeans and a gorgeous black, clinging T-shirt with a silver belt hugging her slim waist. The stiletto heels on her black, open-toe sandals suited her taste in clothes but not the scenery. But it was her hair which caused Susan a moment of jealousy. It was as black as the Japanese princess's but rather than being tied back modestly, this girl's hair was flowing freely down her back to her waist and over her left shoulder. She sat down next to the princess and crossed her legs as Susan expected a model might, then pulling her small black handbag onto her lap she began to study her long, painted finger nails.

She looked like she'd be an interesting person to get to know although there was something about her which made Susan think her Dad would not necessarily approve of a close friendship.

The ferry man hauled the heavy plank up onto the boat and slowly pulled away from the shore. When they were a safe distance out the boat began to turn slowly and Susan found herself gradually turning to face Ness Head.

On the whole, the brief journey from Teignmouth to Shaldon was a quiet one. The children dabbled their hands in the water, and the other passengers kept to themselves. Just two incidents caught everyone's attention. The first was when Peter leant perilously over the side and three people instinctively reached out to grab his leg. The second was the gasp that rose from the passengers when, the fat man leaning forward to say something to the princess, the ferry listed dangerously.

22

Smuggler's Tunnel

All too soon they arrived on Shaldon, unnoticed. The sun shone brightly, a lonely cloud was tiptoeing its way across the sky, and the waves were lapping happily on the sand. It was as if Shaldon were taking a nap. The only sign of any life at all were the seagulls crying as they circled and dived overhead.

Susan was relieved when the fat man get off before her, since the plank bent so much when he stopped on it, that she was afraid it might snap in two. Kathy was escorted off by Dad and Susan, as usual, hang back to capture the moment.

"What! Frogs spawning?" Susan heard the ferryman say to Mum with a chuckle. "My dear lady, you are absolutely right, the pond *is* alive with tadpoles and yes, they *do* divert the traffic but that is in the spring, not in the height of summer. Of course, you will still find one or two frogs in the pond and if you are afraid of the creatures I suggest you take your family up through the village and then turn into Broadlands Botanical Gardens – it'll bring you out onto the top road and, turning left down the hill, you will be able to come at the tunnel from the top."

"What about taking the coastal path?" Dad asked as he joined Mum, linking his arm through hers.

"No – it'll take you over the top of Ness Cove but there aren't any steps leading down to the beach from there," the ferryman answered.

"What's wrong, Susan?" Kathy asked when Susan sat next to her on the wall at the top of the steps.

"Mum's talking to the ferryman about the frogs in the pond," Susan said in dismay. "You know Mum and frogs. Even if there is only one she will be terrified of meeting it on the road, and I really don't want to go on the top road, that's all."

Susan could remember the gaps between the houses which, while providing spectacular views out over the back beach, for someone suffering with agoraphobia, were to be avoided at all costs.

Knowing that her phobia was open spaces and that her Mum's was frogs, she was confounded by her Mum's proposal that just the two of them walk up the main road which followed the sea and swept past The Ness Hotel.

"Hmmm, I don't fancy the long way round any more than you do. As long as you walk first to make sure the frogs don't jump on me I'm sure I'll be fine," Mum said with an attempt at a smile.

"You two are coming with me," Dad said approaching Kathy and Peter, "we'll see if the two ladies can beat us to the top. Mum and Susan are going to check one or two shops first to see if they can find a Whimsey."

Dad pecked Mum on the cheek and, with Kathy and Peter on either side of him, strode away briskly with his usual grin.

"Mum?"

"Yes, Susan?"

"No 'Mother Macree going out to tea'! Okay?"

"Fine! Let's see if we can find you a Whimsey."

There were none. It seemed as if they were going out of fashion, little plastic animals with bobbing heads and big heart-shaped eyes having taken their place.

It must have taken them longer in the shops than they thought because Kathy, Peter and Dad were already sitting outside the entrance to the tunnel. They looked as if they had been sitting there for ages.

"How did you manage that, Darly?"

"We ... a ... walked...ha...quite... fast ... didn't ...we ...kids?"

"Yep."

"It sounds like you have been running the London marathon!"

"Okay," Susan said impatiently. "We're here now. Can we go?"

One thing was certain. She didn't want to waste time nattering about nothing in particular when they could be in the tunnel.

But when Dad stood up, grabbed hold of Mum's hand and headed for the tunnel, Susan begged them to slow down. She knew all too well that if Mum and Dad were in front they would have to walk very fast to keep up and she and Kathy and Peter had all agreed that they didn't want to charge through the tunnel. The previous year they'd pretended to be smuggling gold over to France but this year Peter had asked if they could be detectives on the lookout for kidnappers.

It was a dark, clammy place with walls of uneven slabs of reddish rock and even redder brick and lit by strip lights set in the arched ceiling. Water seeped through the roof and dribbled down the walls leaving damp marks and a musty smell. But it was an excellent place for producing eerie echoes and Peter certainly wasn't going to waste any time before doing so. Mum and Dad were already well into the tunnel by the time the children entered and, with a glance over her shoulder, Mum called back.

"Dad and I are going on ahead. Just remember that other people won't be terribly happy to have to endure your ghostly sounds, Peter. OK?"

"All right, Mum – BYE – BYE – BYE!" Peter's raised voice and the wall's response was enough to encourage their parents to pick up speed.

"HELLO, ANYONE THERE? THERE – THERE? We've got you surrounded – ed ed ed."

"My go, Peter," said Kathy.

"AH – AH – AH. Go on Susan, your turn!" But Susan didn't hear her. She was staring into the depths of the tunnel where her mum and dad were overtaking a little old lady. Dad had stopped to say something to her and, before passing on had shaken hands with the lad who was assisting her. It couldn't be? Or could it?

"Susan! Your turn!"

"SSSH – SSSH –SSSH!" She was getting embarrassed. It was most definitely Lee and his Nan. She was sure that her first encounter with them hadn't left them with a positive impression of her and now she was making echoes in a tunnel with her younger brother and sister. How childish. But what to do? She glanced down at her feet. That morning she'd slipped on her comfortable walking shoes that had no laces so she couldn't use that as her excuse to stop. Thinking quickly, she challenged her brother and sister.

"Who's going to beat me to the end?"

"Me!" and Kathy was off.

"Hey, who thaid you could have a head thtart?" Peter shouted and raced after her.

Susan stooped down to rub her ankle as though she had managed to twist it, only to see both Kathy and Peter charging back towards her.

"I won."

"No, you didn't. I did," Peter panted as he grabbed Susan's arm to stop himself.

"Why didn't you run?" Kathy asked her.

"I must have sprained my ankle when I started," Susan said in despair. "How were the steps down to the beach? Soaking, as usual?"

"We don't know. We didn't get that far. There was a little old lady blocking the path. She's even shorter than Granma and she walks slower, too. But the guy's cute. You should see him!"

"Really?" Susan was caught off guard. She had so wanted to keep Lee a secret and now they'd all seen him. Well, when she saw him, she would just have to pretend she wasn't impressed.

Susan walked as slowly as she could, but the old lady's progress was slower, and soon the time came for them to pass her. So much had happened since the boy had spoken to her in the shop that perhaps he'd forgotten all about her. But clearly not. As they passed, Lee looked straight at her and didn't look away. He was as handsome as she had remembered and his eyes as captivating as they had been the very first time she had gazed into them. Of course, he had kept her company in her dreams each night since then and it was very difficult to remember that the conversations they had had and the walks on the promenade were only part of her imagination. Then she realised he was still looking at her and was waiting for an answer to a question he must have asked her while she had been lost in her thoughts.

"Yeth, we are," Peter answered on her behalf, just as she was casting about for something to say. "Are you on holiday, too?"

"Yes, my Nan lives here and I came to visit. I leave tomorrow though."

"Where do you live?"

"California."

"Really, Wow! Do you thupport the Dodgers?"

"No, the Dodgers are in Los Angeles. I live near San Francisco so I support the Giants."

Peter's pet topic had come in handy because it had given Susan chance to study Lee's Nan. She had blue eyes which had probably once been very beautiful but were now clouding over. Her silvery-gray hair was cut in a stylish bob. Just as Susan remembered her, she was small but elegant. She was holding onto Lee's arm and clutched a smart wooden walking stick with an intricate carving of a swan on one side.

Susan was dying to ask her where she lived but didn't have a chance because, while they talked, they had been approaching the most mysterious part of the tunnel and the point that Susan disliked the most with its three dimly-lit flights of sodden steps leading down and down and down to the mouth of the tunnel. Fortunately there was a sturdy hand rail running the length of both walls to stop people from slipping and Susan grabbed one as she felt her head begin to swim.

Kathy and Peter, having apparently decided that the pace was too slow had begun to hurtle down the steps totally oblivious to any potential danger. This time, when they disappeared from sight, Susan was sure they wouldn't be running all the way back up again. She was alone with her mystery boy and his Nan. And in front of her were the dreaded stairs. Intent on delaying the descent as long as possible, she stepped aside to let them pass.

"Oh no," the old woman said. "After you, my dear. It's a slow climb down for me."

"Be careful," Lee added. "Those steps look slippery."

"Yes, I know. Especially at the bottom. I come here every year. I hope your Nan will be all right."

"I hope so, too," his grandmother said. "I've been coming here for twenty-five years, ever since my husband retired here, but lately the climb seems to get steeper and longer. If we don't make it to the bottom this year, enjoy Ness Cove for me. It really is a charming spot."

With that, Lee and his Nan turned their attention to each step and the distance between them and Susan slowly grew wider. She was leaving her mystery boy behind and possibly the mystery of the view through the window as well.

If only they had a chance to really talk, she thought even though she knew there was no point in wishing. Lee was leaving the next day and her family wouldn't be returning to Teignmouth once their hotel closed. She was sure of that.

Susan reached the bottom step and walked out into the fresh sea air, squinting in the bright sunshine. Just three more short flights of steps down and she'd be in Ness Cove where her mother, already at the far end, was waving to her. Waving back Susan slipped off her shoes and walked onto the sand which was particularly warm after the coolness of the tunnel. For a moment, she paused, lost in the beauty of the spot with its deep cliffs and red rocks where Kathy and Peter were enjoying leaping over the sheltering rock pools. The sea in the cove was an enticing deep aqua marine and the sky – oh the sky – a cloudless, perfect summer day.

Susan made her way carefully between the worm casts which twisted and turned and disappeared when she accidentally stepped on one. A small crab scuttled in front of her and she stooped down to pick up a delicate pink round shell with a shiny mother of pearl wrapped inside.

It was going to be a hot day, even the seagulls were lazy here, one or two strutting on the sand and the remaining bobbing on the gently waves. Only one family was in the cove, a young couple with a naked little child happily digging near his mother.

It was good to discover that the cove was basically theirs for the day.

They hadn't brought much with them, a couple of beach towels to sit on and a picnic lunch, courtesy of the hotel. And, of course, books for Mum and Dad. Susan retrieved the notebook she had slipped inside Dad's rucksack and flopped down on her tummy on a spare towel, determined to make a note of what had happened so that she would never forget the moment. As she wriggled her body to make a comfortable indent in the sand beneath her she caught sight of Lee and his Nan appearing at the mouth of the tunnel. She watched as he handed his Nan her stick and stood beside her at the top of the steps which Susan had just come down, looking out to sea.

When Lee raised an arm and pointed to the horizon, Susan turned and saw a tall ship, a galleon similar to one of the models she had made a couple of Christmases before.

But when she looked back to Lee her heart sank. They weren't coming down to the cove after all. Instead, they had turned and were making their way back into the tunnel.

"Goodbye, my mystery boy," Susan whispered and felt one single tear trickle down her cheek.

23

The Crab

Peter's ear piercing scream woke Mum up and got Dad jumping up from his towel in record timing. The scream lasted until Dad got to the rock pool that Peter had slipped into.

"Ow, get it off, get it off!"

Susan ran over to join them.

"What happened, Kathy?"

"We were sitting on this rock dangling our toes in the water and that happened!" Kathy said, laughing.

Susan looked down to see Dad attempting to pry a large crab, that was holding on for dear life, off Peter's big toe!

"Ow, it hurtth, Dad," Peter cried. "Get it off."

"Hold on, son. And please try to stop waving your leg around!"

"I hope Mum brought some plasters," Susan said, seeing a dribble of blood on Peter's foot.

"You've got to be kidding," Kathy said. "Of course, she won't have."

"Well, we'd better think of something quick," Dad said. "Find a branch with twigs on it. We can use them. Hurry up. There's always wood on a beach, swept in from wreckages and storms."

"Have you got it off yet, Dad?" Peter whined.

"No. It won't move."

"I can't find any wood," Kathy yelled.

When Susan clambered off the rocks and reached her sister at the bottom of the cliff, she found that Kathy had been right. There wasn't any wood, but there were bushes. Tugging at one prickly branch until it came loose, she took it to Dad who put it down the small gap between the crab's fore-pincer and Peter's poor toe. After manoeuvring it for a painful second or two, he pulled it back, and sure enough, there was his prey dangling on the branch.

Peter, whose toe certainly looked battered, hadn't managed to hold back his tears. Clinging to Susan, he limped his way over the rocks and then hopped back to Mum, trying to keep his foot out of the sand while she rummaged in the picnic basket and found a paper napkin which she tenderly wrapped round the bleeding toe after which she wrapped her arms round her youngest and he sat quietly with her for a few minutes. But it wasn't long before he was joking about his crab.

"Do you reckon I could catch a shark with my toe now it'th all bloody?" he said.

"Peter!"

"I wathn't thwearing, Mum. I wath jutht talking about my bloody toe!"

"Peter, that's enough!"

"Yeth, Dad!"

Crab, Crab, on my toe!
Pull it off?
Yeth!
There you go!

After Mum poured orange juice into plastic cups for the children and cups of steaming tea for herself and Dad, she handed round cheese and cucumber sandwiches and Kathy and Peter, grabbing theirs, dashed off back to the rock pools, Peter clearing having forgotten all about his toe. Ness Cove became what it always had been – a peaceful spot for escaping from the crowds – a day of being together, with everyone free to explore or just lounge about.

"Mum, did you bring the sun cream?" Susan asked. There was a lovely gentle breeze, but as Susan had rubbed the sand off her thigh she had felt the unmistakable and unpleasant sensation of sunburn. That was unusual for her since she usually went a deep golden brown without too much aid from the lotions.

"Yes, here you are. Would you mind doing my shoulders for me, too?"

"Of course, not. Did you put cream on Kathy, Mum?"

"Do you know what, Susan? No I didn't. Go and call her, would you. There's a good girl."

"Mum!" Susan sighed. The last thing she wanted right now was to go traipsing off in search of her brother and sister. "She's right at the end of the bay. Look!"

"Where?"

"There!"

"What – you mean those two little spots, but they were right here a minute ago!"

"Yes. Those two little spots."

"Oh, Darly. Do you think you could call Peter and Kathy back – they're almost out of sight."

"Tunky! Relax!"

Since Dad's head didn't appear over his book as it usually did, Susan wasn't certain that he had heard. Susan guessed it must be a really good book and tried to read the title; *Virgil's Aeneid.* Hmmm! That didn't sound terribly enthralling.

"She's bound to be back soon and we'll put cream on then," said Mum turning on to her tummy and resting her head on her arms. That was Mum taken care of. Susan knew she wouldn't stir for ages.

The next few hours passed without event. The family with the little boy left and a man with a camera took their place and began to take shot after shot of the cove. Mum and Dad didn't stir and Susan used the time to write in her book and do a sketch.

Since Ness Cove faced east, the sun always disappeared from the beach by mid-afternoon, but it still remained lovely and warm for a couple more hours. It wasn't until it began to get cooler that Dad dropped his book in his lap, looked up and stretched.

"Where is everyone?" he said. "Ready to go?"

"Well, Mum and I are here and Peter and Kathy somewhere over there!" said Susan pointing in the vague direction of the rock pools.

"Right, go and call them, please, Suz. Tunky, we need to be making a move."

"So soon?" Mum said, lazily opening her eyes and yawning.

The minute Susan stood up, she knew that she was in trouble. Her shoulders were stinging and she realized she was burned. Badly. And if that was the case for her, Kathy was going to be in major trouble.

24

Sunstroke

Kathy was ten times blonder than Susan and Peter and burned ten times more easily. But even knowing that, Susan was not prepared for what she saw when Kathy came into sight. Her sister had stripped off to her swimming costume and every part of her body that the sun could touch had changed to a bright red making the whites of her eyes looking ghostly by contrast.

"Kathy, I hate to tell you this, but you're awfully burned," she said, appalled.

"Really?" Kathy did not seem to be particularly concerned. "We've been having so much fun. Look!"

Taking Susan by the hand, Kathy led her to a pool where Susan could see at least six big crabs, numerous mussels and a whole pile of winkles. Peter was prodding one of the crabs with a stick. Susan noticed that his shoulders had caught the sun too but he was nowhere as bad as Kathy. Why, she wondered, wasn't she complaining?

"Get a move on, you two," she said. "We need to go."

"Can't we have another few minutes?"

"I don't think so. Dad is already packing up. Come on."

Kathy picked up her T-shirt and shorts which were lying crumpled on a rock and started back to Mum and Dad. As she was walking she slipped her shorts on and Susan noticed her flinch as she pulled them over her hips. The T-shirt proved impossible but Kathy chose to suffer in silence.

"Oh, my darling. Look at you!" Mum cried. "How could I have been so foolish? I should have called you back to put cream on you. That breeze was deceptive. Come here, sweetheart. I can't put cream on you now but we'll use some cool towels when we get back to the hotel. How do you feel?"

"My head feels funny," Kathy's voice sounded slurred and Dad looked alarmed.

"Come on K-Jdlums – hold my hand."

It was a real struggle for Kathy to get back up the steps. Susan saw her feet slip several times and Dad's arm tighten round her. By the time they got to the top, Kathy looked pale, despite her sunburn, and Dad half supported, half carried her through the tunnel and back down to the main street.

It was a good fifteen minutes before the ferry arrived. There was nothing romantic about the trip this time and Susan, who was beginning to get a headache, wasn't at all interested in the other passengers. She knew the ferryman was talking to Mum but she couldn't hear what they were saying and she wasn't terribly bothered.

Kathy cried out in pain as she sat in the car and couldn't rest her back against the seat. So, she sat forward instead with her head in her hands. Susan leant her head against the window on her side and shut her eyes What a good thing they had chosen to bring the car after all. Her head was pounding and she wished Peter would stop talking about crabs. It wasn't until they turned into the car park behind the hotel that Susan opened her eyes a little and knew that she was not very well.

Nanny happened to be in the lobby as the family entered.

"My goodness dearies! What happened to you today? I'll just run and get some cold cloths. Mrs. Thomas, you're going to need to get your two girls into bed, I fear. How about me looking after Peter for you for a while?"

"Thank you, Nanny. That would be a big help. Are we in time for tea?"

"Don't you go worrying about a thing. I'll have your table made up in a jiffy. You both look like you could do with a cuppa."

"Oh, that sounds lovely," Mum answered with a sigh.

"This way, Peter," Nanny said. "Come and tell me what you've been up to today and all about why you're limping."

Peter left cheerfully with Nanny, and Susan and Mum followed Dad, who was carrying Kathy, who was now limp and listless, in his arms.

Somewhere between the hall and the bedroom Susan lost awareness of what was going on around her and it wasn't until it was dark that she woke with a start. The lights in the room were off and the curtains were drawn back slightly letting the cool night air in through the open window. There were snuffling noises coming from Kathy's side of the room but Susan wasn't able to work out whether or not Peter, Mum and Dad were also in bed.

What she *was* aware of, were the huge spiders that were walking all over the ceiling and the one that was crawling down the wall towards her bed. Susan dived under her sheet only to come face to face with a furry tarantula which was creeping up her arm. She started to scream, but didn't dare because she was afraid that the monster might crawl inside her mouth. But by now she was near panic and her shriek brought Mum and Dad to the bedside immediately.

Mum soothed her by placing a cool, damp flannel on her forehead and Dad put the bedside lamp on and poured her a glass of water lifting her head slightly and getting her to take a sip.

"You've got sunstroke, Suz," he said as a dribble trickled down her neck. "The spiders aren't real. Try and fall asleep again. The doctor will be back in the morning."

Having Mum's hand on her forehead was reassuring and knowing that she would keep the spiders away, Susan drifted off.

25

Steven's Visit

Morning brought more sun and the doctor.

"You are both very lucky young ladies," he said, as he put his thermometer back into his bag. "Another hour in the sun and both of you would both have had to spend the night in hospital. Now listen carefully. There is to be no beach for you today. I want you both to stay out of the sun for twenty-four hours. And you are to drink water – plenty of water. Any nonsense and I will send my ambulance to get you. Understand?"

The girls nodded in unison. Susan knew that Kathy was no more interested in being hospitalized than she was.

"Nanny has agreed to listen out for you on the monitor," the doctor confirmed "and I suggest, Sir, that you take your wife and son and go out for a few hours so that the girls can get some rest. I'll be back again in the evening to make sure your daughters are comfortable for the night."

"What about Kathy's sunburn?" asked Mum.

"Keep doing what you've been doing since yesterday. Cool, damp towels and lots of water. I'll bring some special cream this evening. In the meantime, give her this to keep the temperature down. And there's one more thing. Kathy, here is beginning to blister. Whatever you do – don't let her burst the bubbles and don't let her peel the skin off when it begins to flake."

"That'll be tough." Mum told him. "If there's one thing Kathy loves to do it's pulling her skin off!"

"Well, she mustn't!" said the doctor sternly. "I don't want her in hospital anymore than you do."

After the doctor left, Nanny arrived with a pot of tea and a plate of biscuits, and a short while later Dad ushered Mum and Peter out of the room, assuring the girls that they wouldn't be long. As for Nanny, she popped her head round the door every ten to fifteen minutes to let them know they hadn't been deserted. Susan and Kathy drifted in and out of sleep and were both surprised when Dad came in saying it was one o'clock and that they were back for dinner.

"Can I get anything for the two of you?" he asked anxiously.

Susan sat up in bed. "Can I get up now. I am feeling much better."

"Have you been drinking water?"

"Yes, Dad. I'm getting sick of the stuff. What's for dinner?"

"Fish and chips."

"Oh, Dad, *please* can I have fish and chips. I'm famished."

"I'll go and see what Nanny says. What about you, Kiff? Want anything?"

Kathy looked up at him from under burnt eyelids.

"Ice-cream? Can I have some ice-cream?"

"Your wish is my command."

Susan was sitting on Kathy's bed with her notebook on her knee when Dad returned bringing fish and chips for everyone except Kathy who was still munching away happily on her ice cream.

It was the sight of fish and chips which caused Susan to throw her book down rather than the fear that her father might ask her what she was writing.

"You both gave us a scare yesterday but I am glad to see you're both picking up," Dad said. "Are you feeling up to having a visitor this afternoon?"

Kathy and Susan looked at each other curiously.

"Who?" they said in unison.

"Steven. He's been hovering outside your door all morning. I told him I'd ask you first."

"How do I look, Dad?" Kathy fretted, running her fingers through her hair.

"Well, you could win a prize for the most beautiful red Indian I've ever seen," he said cheerfully. "I won't let him stay long but I think he's got something to give you."

"Give me time to get dressed first." Susan mumbled, her mouth full of fish and chips. How she wished it was Lee coming to see her instead. Oh, but of course, he had left for California while she'd been asleep.

Finishing her dinner hastily, Susan slipped a T-shirt on and some shorts, relieved to see that her legs were a lovely golden brown. She was fortunate to tan so easily although twisting her head round she knew that her shoulders hadn't been so lucky. But at least they weren't stinging as badly as the previous day.

Mum came in to collect the plates and to tell the girls that they could get up if they promised to take it easy. She seemed surprised to see Susan dressed.

"Up already! I thought you'd be cuddled up in bed still!"

"This might be our last time in Teignmouth," Susan told her. "I'm not going to spend it in bed."

"That may be. But you're not going down to the beach!"

"Yes, I know. I heard what the doctor said."

"Right. We are going to take Peter along to Parson's tunnel this afternoon. If you need anything press this button here by the window."

"Can we go to the pier later?"

"You! On the pier! Since when have you ever wanted to go on the pier?"

"Please?"

"I'm not promising anything. We'll have to wait and see what the doctor says when he comes at five. Now, if you are ready Steven is waiting outside the door. Can I send him in?"

"I'm decent," Susan said. But Kathy's leg is uncovered. You don't want to encourage him too much!"

"Oh, shut up, Susan!"

When Mum opened the door Steven almost fell in!

Steven walked in boldly as Mum went out, saying that she'd be back in a few minutes. His head held high, his shoulders back, his hair neatly combed and a dark blue shirt tucked tidily into what looked like a new pair of jeans.

Susan was gobsmacked. Could this be the kid they had tried so desperately to get rid of the previous year. What had happened to him? Granted, he was still as skinny as a rail but it wasn't the same boy.

"I'm sorry you're sick," he said, going to stand beside Susan. "I thought you might like a stick of rock. I saw some of the pictures you've done and I thought maybe you could copy the picture on the label-."

"Oh, thanks, Steven," Susan replied. "It's just the kind of picture I like to draw."

She was, she found, genuinely touched. The small photo of Teignmouth pier wrapped round the stick would make an ideal sketch.

Steven had clearly finished with her because he quickly turned to Kathy and took out a small package from his pocket.

"It reminded me of you," was all Susan caught before Mum came back in to get her handbag and put some cream on her shoulders.

"I'm sorry, Steven," she said briskly. "Time's up. Doctor's orders. The girls are supposed to rest again."

"No problem, Mrs. Thomas," he replied. "Mum's waiting for me downstairs. She's going to take me over to Shaldon."

"Just one piece of advice, Steven," Mum added. "Take a hat if you've got one and use lots of sun cream so you don't end up like the girls."

"I'll do that, Mrs. Thomas," he said earnestly, adding as he turned back to the two girls, "I hope you both get well soon."

Once he was gone, Mum went to each girl in turn, feeling the backs of their necks and pouring some more water into their glasses before she disappeared again. Susan and Kathy raced as quickly as their burns allowed to the window, hoping to catch a glimpse of Steven's Mum.

They were just in time. Steven, head still held high, turned on the bottom step and held out his hand to a woman coming to join him. The girls could see he was beaming from ear to ear.

"No way!" whispered Kathy, as the two turned back to look at the hotel. "See who it is!"

"You've got to be kidding!" Susan exclaimed. "That's Steven's mother? Oh, my goodness!"

It was the model used in the Soft Shampoo commercial. Her long auburn hair, cascading down her back, glowed in the summer afternoon sunshine and she had on the most gorgeous summer dress in various shades of green which showed off her perfect slim figure. Susan had never seen such long legs nor such high heels.

"Wow. Look at how she walks, Susan! Isn't that incredible. She looks just the way she does on the telly."

Kathy was right. Steven's mum walked with poise and grace. Her suntan put Susan's to shame and her face was the face of an angel; radiant and alive and happy. She was very obviously content and her son – well, Susan understood now why he was a different boy. But what a contrast between his goddess mother and his ogre of a father.

Hand in hand, they crossed the road to the promenade, heads turning as she passed. Even cars slowed down and drivers beeped their horns. One went past her with two lads hanging out of windows, waving and wolf-whistling.

Neither Kathy nor Susan spoke as they knelt on Susan's bed, noses pressed on the glass watching until mother and son walked out of sight. Then, still without a word, they turned round and sat staring at each other.

"Well, well, well!" Susan said eventually. "Who would have thought it? What did he give you, Kathy?"

"This," her sister said, opening her clasped hand. On her palm was a delicate Whimsey sea horse, perfect in every detail.

"Oh, Kathy! It's beautiful," Susan exclaimed. It was one of the Whimsey's she had hoped to find for her collection. "I wonder where he bought it?"

After the two girls had admired the tiny sea horse, Kathy yawned, and curling up, with it still clenched in one hand, went to sleep.

As for Susan, she was glad to have some time to herself. Sitting by the window, she let her mind wander from Lee to Steven, Steven's mum and dad, the fat man and his Japanese princess, Peter's crab and Kathy's sea-horse. How long had they been in Teignmouth? She'd lost count. Soon it would be time to go home.

26

The Mist Returns

Leaving Kathy snoring, Susan went to the bathroom. When she returned to their room, and shut the door behind her, she froze. Something very strange was happening to the window just above her bed.

Despite the fact that it was sunny out, the window was beginning to mist over, very slowly, from the bottom left hand corner. The mist moved gradually to the middle and then higher until the whole window looked like frosted glass. First the chaotic sand and seagulls, then Lee and the door in the wall and now this was happening again. She didn't know if she wanted to look this time but curiosity eventually got the better of her. She crawled onto her bed and rubbed a hole in the mist about the size of a ten pence piece. Then, closing her left eye, she took a peek with her right.

A solitary tree, with a rickety, old wooden chair leaning up against it, stood in what looked like a courtyard. A dark little girl in a pretty yellow dress with a yellow ribbon in her hair, her face tear-stained, sat holding a balloon on her lap.

Susan made the hole bigger and the picture grew with it. Several other children, dressed smartly but running barefoot, were playing with cardboard boxes. Certainly it was not England.

The building on the left was whitewashed and had what looked like turrets running round the top. The windows were just holes in the wall, with wooden shutters, paint peeling along the edges, hanging loosely from rusty hinges. Susan saw a little boy slither down a rusty slide on the right and land smack on his bottom in a pool of dust, but he didn't even seem to notice, let alone mind.

Kathy coughed in her sleep, and Susan, relieved that she was not awake, turned back to the window and found herself looking at Teignmouth promenade where Mum and Dad were waiting to cross the road. Overwhelmed with disappointment that the little girl was no longer there, Susan threw herself onto her bed. Had she imagined it all? But no, she was sure that she had not. What was happening?

At that moment the door burst open and Peter charged in. "Thuthan, Thuthan, gueth who we thaw! Where are you? Oh, you're in bed. We thaw you in the window. Did you thee uth?"

"Peter, I was asleep," said Kathy with a yawn. "When will you learn to be quieter?"

"Peter, I thought we told you to come in quietly," Dad said as he strode over to the window and looked out. "How are you feeling, girls?"

"Fine, Dad," Kathy told him. "Honestly I do. Can we go to the pier this evening?"

"Oh, no," Peter protested. "Not the pier. Can't we go to Parthon'th tunnel again. We almotht got blown off the wall by an interthity. You haven't guethed who we thaw. You'll never gueth, will they, Mum?"

"Was she tall, beautiful, with long auburn hair, a beautiful green dress and very high heels?" asked Susan.

"Yeth! But I bet you don't know who she ith!" said Peter.

"Oh, go on. Tell us!"

"She'th Thteven'th mum and she'th really nithe. She bought me an ithe-cream. Thteven thayth she'th filming on the beach tomorrow and we can all go him and watch with the director – if you're feeling better. But we've got to promithe to be ..."

"Peter, I don't know if the girls are going to be well enough tomorrow," Mum interrupted him.

But by that stage both Kathy and Susan were showing remarkable signs of having miraculously recovered.

Mum noticed!

"We'll ask the doctor when he comes," she said. "In fact, he'll be here any moment. Kathy, why don't you get yourself dressed and maybe he'll say it's possible for us all to go down for tea together."

As if by clockwork, there was a knock on the door and the doctor appeared as if on cue. This time his visit was a quick one. Seeing Susan up and dressed and Kathy clearly rested he said "Yes" to tea time and "Yes" to the beach the following day – as long as it was for a short time and providing they wore sunhats and sun-cream.

27

Message in a Bottle

At tea time everyone waited for Steve's mum to arrive but there were no signs of either of them. When they'd almost finished eating Mum looked at Dad with dreamy eyes and when he nodded, Susan knew that they wanted to say something to them.

"Goodness, I hope they're not going to tell us they are expecting a baby!" she thought to herself. But she didn't need to worry about smelly nappies for long because they simply wanted to tell their children that tonight was the night they usually went over to Shaldon for their dinner dance.

"If you think you can cope without us this evening, girls, I'd like to take Mum over to Shaldon," Dad said, grinning. "What do you think? Will you cope?"

The girls looked at each other and Susan knew the twinkle in her eyes would not go unnoticed.

"Susan!"

"Yes, Dad? Of course we don't mind if you go. Um... Kathy and I can plan what we'll wear down on the beach tomorrow when they're filming."

"What about me? moaned Peter. Do I have to thtay with them. I might catch their bug."

"It's not a bug you can catch," said Mum reassuringly, "and no, you do not have to spend all evening in the room. You can go down to the games room and Nanny will tell you when it's time to come back up."

Watching Mum get dressed up for the dance later was like spying on Cinderella getting ready for the ball. But in this case her prince was standing next to her ready and willing to run her zip all the way from her waist to the nape of her neck. It was a lovely long, low-cut dress and the girls pleaded with her to do a twirl. As the delicate silk material swirled round with her, Dad deftly caught her hand and with a quick 1-2-3 waltzed her round the room. He looked stunning in his black tuxedo and Susan could see why Mum had fallen head over heels in love with him. Lee was just as gorgeous, she thought.

Mum picked up her sparkly handbag, opened it and took out a minute glass bottle, dabbed perfume behind her ears, and applied lipstick sparingly. Pronouncing herself ready, she slipped her arm through Dad's and glided out of the door.

"Now?" asked Kathy.

"Wait a minute! Pete, darling?" Susan said. "Aren't you going down to the games room?" stalling her eager sister.

"That dependth."

"On what?"

"Thuthan, thinth when have you ever planned what you are going to wear to the beach?" he said suspiciously.

"You cheeky beggar! How often do we have the chance to be near TV cameras?"

"Oh, tho you really are going to talk about girly thtuff?"

"Well, actually. Shall we tell him, Kathy?"

"Oh, all right," Kathy nodded.

"While you were out this morning Kathy and I came up with a good idea,"

"Another one?"

"Yep!" said Kathy. "Susan's written a message to put in a bottle and we are going to throw it in the sea tomorrow and see if anyone gets it before we leave."

"Really? Can I read it?"

"It's not quite finished yet. Kathy, throw me my notebook. It should be on your bed somewhere."

"Here it is," said Kathy and she began to flick through the pages.

"Give it to me," Susan snapped.

"Wow. Susan it's amazing. Look, Peter."

Susan jumped off her bed, dashed to where her brother and sister were studying the sketch she had drawn while they were in Ness Cove, and grabbed her precious notebook from Kathy's hand.

"Flippin' eck. We were only looking."

"Well, don't!" Susan retreated to her side of the room and held the picture up to look at. She had managed to capture on paper the view through the top landing window and as she glanced she thought she saw Lee walking out through the patio door.

"It's even better than the one you did of our house. Where is it?"

"I drew it from my imagination."

"I wish I could draw like that!"

Susan relaxed. She actually liked it when people said her pictures were amazing. At least she had something she was good at. She had been terrified that they would turn to the next page where she had written a love letter to Lee. That, she wouldn't have been able to explain as easily.

"Here it is," quickly changing subjects.   She had found the page with the message.

If you find this bottle come to the East Cliff end of
Teignmouth Promenade at 10pm.
Stand under the last lamp post
We will be watching out for you.

"What if an old drunk man findth it? Or thomebody grumpy like Farty Gerty or a kidnapper?" said Peter, eyes blazing with excitement.

"Where *do* you get your ideas from?" asked Susan.

"I dunno. Maybe my imagination! Listen to this. I've got a poem!"

Write a note
Put it in the bottle
If you find it
Come to the hotel."

Peter said hotel to rhyme with bottle and Susan and Kathy sniggered.

"You're good, Peter!" Susan picked up her pen and started to chew the end. "You've given me an idea though. We need to make sure that the person is about our age to make it more fun. Why don't we write a P.S, something like:

"If you are older than sixteen give the bottle to the next person you see who is under sixteen."

They all agreed that it was a good note and scoured the room for a bottle, but without any luck.

"I'll get you one," said Peter, "glath or plathtic?"

"What do you think, Kiff?"

"I don't know!"

"Gosh, girlth are uthleth!" Peter said, with a sigh and a shrug. "I'll get one of each and you can choothe."

He was gone too quickly for Susan and Kathy to ask him where he was going and returned in such record timing that they knew he couldn't have gone very far. Puffing and panting, he held out both hands. In one was a plastic bottle that had the remains of a sticky red drink. When Kathy unscrewed the lid, she held the bottle at arm's length and pinched her nose.

"Phew!" she said. "I think it's fermentated!"

"Fermented, Kathy!"

"That, too!"

The second bottle was made of dark green glass but was without a cork, so they discarded it by rolling it under Peter's bed.

"Hope Dad doesn't find it!"

"I can take it back later on," offered Peter, who unfortunately promptly forgot all about it.

Susan rinsed out the plastic bottle, putting a spot of Mum's shampoo in and shaking it up and down furiously to get rid of the smell, and then spent the next few minutes attempting to get the soap suds out until the bottle was finally clean and dry.

After Kathy copied the note on a piece of paper they got from Dad's brief case, Susan rolled it expertly and popped it in. Then screwing the lid on, she looked round for somewhere to put it till the next day, finally settling on the bedside cupboard next to her bed behind a pile of T-shirts, at which point, Kathy, saying that she felt a bit woozy, got into her pyjamas and was soon asleep. As for Susan, she busied herself recording what she had seen beyond the window and Peter, soon bored by the lack of activity, headed for the games room.

By the time Mum and Dad returned a few hours later it was to reports from Nanny of their perfectly well-brought up children.

"I'm going to miss them which I head back to Buntingford," she'd told them. "They're special children. They really are."

Susan wasn't terribly sure that she liked the implication of being special and well-brought up, expecting it would mean she would have to try not to ever risk disappointing her parents. Well, as long as it didn't equate to being boring she thought she might be able to manage. At least she would try.

28

The Bottle Returns

The following morning was different from every other morning they had ever awakened to in Teignmouth. Outside their windows the ordinarily peaceful promenade had been transformed into a bustling film set. Men were scurrying everywhere, setting up cameras and lights and backdrops. There were caravans parked along the curb. Policemen were directing traffic and, of course, interested tourists milling around, were beginning to form a crowd.

A small stage had been erected on their spot on the beach and, despite the excitement of knowing it was all because of Steven's mum, the children were sad that it couldn't all be happening just a few meters further down the beach.

Just then they were distracted by the sound of loud voices in the corridor. One of them, Susan thought, sounded like Steven's father, and the woman's must be his mother's. Peter was trying to see through the keyhole when someone tapped, and the children found themselves face to face with Steven and an older gentleman who was most certainly *not* his father.

"Here they are," Steven said. "These are the friends I told Mum about."

"Right, lad." The man stuck his head round the door.

"I'm sorry to disturb you all at this early hour," he said. "Miss Lister would like to invite your three children to the filming session today," he said after he and Dad, who was now in his dressing gown, had shaken hands, "but they will need your written permission and I'll need a few details, if I may."

"Of course," said Dad cheerfully, and added, "I have a feeling they would be delighted."

"Good. I'll wait for you down in the reception hall with all the necessary documents."

"See you later!" Steven said as they left the room.

"We don't need to tell you to be on your best behaviour, do we?" Dad warned them. "That goes for you too, Peter!"

"Of course not," Susan exclaimed. "We'll all keep low profiles!"

"I think keeping low profiles will be a little hard with so many cameras around!" Dad said with a grin. "Just don't do anything to embarrass yourselves – or us, for that matter!"

As Susan was getting dressed she felt behind her T-shirts just to make sure the bottle was still there. It would be a shame not to throw it in the sea after all the bother they'd gone to. Maybe there would be a moment later on. No, they couldn't do it later. It was now or never.

When Dad left the room to meet the producer, or whoever he was, and Mum snuggled back down under the covers, Susan asked if it was all right if they went down to the beach to watch the television crew set up.

"What time it is?" she yawned.

"Twenty-five to eight."

"Yes, you can. Ask Daddy to take you across the road and be careful when you come back for breakfast."

"Mum, I'm thirteen years old!" Susan protested.

"Yes, I am well aware of that dear, but Peter isn't!"

When Mum disappeared back under the covers Susan was able to get the bottle out without her seeing it and asking tricky questions.

"Can I throw it, Thuthan?" Peter asked as they hurtled down the stairs. "I can throw a cricket ball further than either of you two!"

Susan looked at Kathy.

"I guess so."

Mrs. Gerty glared at the children from behind her desk as they skidded to a walk. Pretending not to see her gesturing to them, the children, determined not to let her spoil the last few days, hurried outside. Fortunately Dad and the man were nowhere to be seen so they were spared the task of explaining what they were up to.

Holding Peter by the shoulder, Susan saw him and Kathy safely across the road to the beach where they jumped off the steps onto the sand and headed straight for the edge of the water.

The tide was lower this morning and there was a stronger breeze than usual. So much so, in fact, that Susan wished she'd slipped her jumper over her T-shirt and shorts.

Facing the pier Susan handed Peter the bottle and he flung it as hard as he could out into the bay. It bobbed on the water, bouncing gently up and down as it went over each new wave.

They had been watching it for a couple of minutes when Steven joined them.

"Are you waiting for that bottle to come ashore?" he said.

"No," Kathy replied. "Peter threw it in!"

"Really! So why is it coming back this way?"

Susan had already realized that their bottle was getting closer to the shore with each wave but hadn't wanted to admit failure so early on.

"That was the first throw," she told him. "Now it's Kathy's turn."

When the bottle floated close enough, Kathy caught hold of it before it slipped out of reach again and threw it out even further, a feat that didn't seem to impress Peter, although Kathy rubbed her hands in glee.

Sadly, the bottle bobbed back to the children once again, and after five minutes they fished it back out for the second time.

"Can I have a try?" Steven asked them.

"Only if you've got a dinghy and can sail out about two hundred meters," Susan answered, frustrated to the extreme. "No, Steven. There's no point. We'll try and drop it off the end of the pier later."

"Hey, the camera man – his name's Chris – said he's going to take some shots of Mum on the pier later. Maybe we could go with them."

"I don't know. We're not supposed to be out for very long today – not after yesterday."

"I'm going to be going," Steven told them, "and Peter isn't sick. So we could do it together."

Susan enjoyed playing her own pranks, but she quickly came to the conclusion that Steven's suggestion actually made sense. The last time she'd attempted to walk on the Grand Pier she'd been conscious of the water moving a long way beneath her as she stepped from plank to plank trying desperately not to look down, but not succeeding. She'd vowed then that she wouldn't do piers again.

"Okay. Here you are," she said, handing Steven the bottle. "Please, promise you won't forget. We've only got a few more days and it would be fun to see who gets it. Come on, you guys. We'd better get back for breakfast. Our prunes await!"

"Do you know what?" Kathy announced. "I've had enough prunes!"

"I know what you mean!" Susan replied.

"Do you want a prune poem?" Peter asked. "It's pretty dithguthting though!"

"No, Peter. I think we could do without a prune poem, thank you very much!"

Prunes it was, and prunes it would be for at least a few more mornings. Kathy and Peter, with expressions of disgust, dispatched them as quickly as possible, although Susan, who still rather liked them, although she was certainly not going to say so, took rather more time.

"Kathy," Mum said, "the doctor had hoped to check your sunburn this morning. When he popped in he was quite surprised to find that you were up and about. Before you and Susan dash off to the filming session make sure you find me so that I can put on some of the cream that he gave me. And – um, girls. Don't forget. It's hats today!"

"You have got to be kidding," Susan said, scowling. "Have you seen how many cameras are out there? I don't want to be filmed wearing a sun hat!"

"It was the doctor's orders," her mother said sternly. "Not mine. No hat – no beach!"

"That's just great!"

"It's not that bad, Sis," Kathy reassured her. "It's better than sitting in the hotel and watching everything through the window."

"Have you seen my new hat, Kathy?"

"What – the big floppy one that makes you look like an elephant in a nappy?"

"Really!" Peter joined in. "I didn't know elephanthth wore nappieth on their headth!"

"You guys, shut up," Susan snapped. "You're no help at all!"

Just then Steven came into the dining room out of breath. "Mr. Chris says he wants to make the most of the early morning sun. Are you ready?"

"We'll be right with you. Mum, if we've got to do this creaming session can we do it now?"

Hat or no hat, Susan was eager not to miss anything. Maybe she'd be spotted by an agent. Then again, maybe not!

29

Miss Lister and the Film Crew

Creamed and suitably covered, the four children met in the lobby where the producer handed each of them an identification badge.

"Miss Lister will be down in just a minute," he said. "If you'd like to, you can wait and go across with her."

"Oh, Yeth pleathe," Peter exclaimed, and Kathy joined in. As for Susan, she was still so embarrassed about having to wear her "big flop," as Kathy called it, that, for once, she didn't have much to say.

And then, there she was coming down the stairs wearing an extremely short, tightly fitting red dress with shoes to match, her long auburn hair swept over her shoulder, a cute body guard on either side of her looking left and right as they entered the reception hall.

"Look at Gerty!" Susan whispered, nudging her sister. Granted that Mrs. Gerty's smile was more like a painful grin, but it was a smile, nevertheless. But seeing the sisters looking at her, she reverted to her usual scowl and went back to examining her books.

When Steven's mother reached them, she kissed him on his forehead and then shook hands with each of them in turn. It was then that Susan realized that she was more than just a model doing a shampoo commercial. She had seen her face somewhere before, but where, she couldn't recall.

"I'm glad Steven has made some friends this holiday," she said. "Thank you. I hope you enjoy today."

And that was all there was time for before she was ushered out of the door and across the street where police had already halted traffic. The children wasted no time in joining the procession down to *their* spot on the beach.

"This way please," said a highly efficient-looking woman holding a black clip board, glasses perched on the tip of her nose.

The children sat where they were told to and watched while Miss Lister was given instructions as to what to do, where to stand, how high to hold her chin and what to do with her hair. It was all very interesting. Mr. Chris bent this way and that to get the best shot. Camera vertical, then horizontal, waving his hand at her as he clicked away and she moved agilely round the stage smiling sweetly.

At one moment, a seagull sat on the chair next to her and Mr. Chris turned his attention to the bird for a moment or two before it flapped its wings and lifted off slowly.

The session went on and on and on until the children began to fidget in their seats and look around. They had finished their water long since and were desperate to stand up and walk over to a table where a girl was handing out what looked like pink lemonade.

When, eventually, Mr. Chris called for a break, Miss Lister rubbed her neck, gathered up all her hair in a high bun and called someone over to massage her shoulders for her.

"If you will come with me," the woman with the clipboard said, "I will get you something to drink." They obediently followed.

"This ith tho boring," said Peter. "Can't we go now?"

"I'm not sure," answered Susan unsure as to what they could and couldn't do, nor how much longer the session was supposed to last. "Let's find Steven. Maybe he'll know."

Steven, who had been talking with Mr. Chris, readily joined them.

"Isn't it great! Chris says he's got some fantastic shots. How would you all like to have a photo taken with me and Mum. I'm sure she wouldn't mind?"

"Can we really?" Kathy asked, and although she was clearly excited, Susan guessed that she was sicker than anyone looking at her might think.

"Yes? Susan?" asked Steven.

"Well, yes," Susan said, "as long as she doesn't mind. But then we ought to be getting back to the hotel. The doctor said we shouldn't stay out too long today and I think Kathy should be lying down."

"Thankth, Thuthan. You're a life thaver!" Peter said, when Steven went to ask his mum.

"I have to say that I thought the life of a model was more interesting than just twisting your head round," Susan admitted. "What about if we get the bottle from Steven and go and throw it ourselves? Kathy, you really do need to go back to the hotel. You look awful. Would you mind if Peter and I went together?"

"I don't mind," her sister said. "I just want to climb into bed and rest awhile."

That was so unlike Kathy that Susan knew she wasn't feeling at all well.

"I'll get the bottle," Peter said. "Steven left it under his chair."

"Thanks, Pete. I'll take Kiff back to the hotel. Come on, Kiff"

"Where are you going?" Steven asked just as the girls started to leave. "My Mum says it's fine with her but could we do it in the evening after she finishes her session?"

"Oh, good! Yes, of course. No problem," Susan told him. "Maybe Kathy will be feeling better by then."

"Oh, please feel better. Please!" Steven begged. "We won't do it if you're not in the photo!"

"Back so soon?" Dad asked, looking up from his book as they came back into the room. "Oh, my! K-Jdlums it's time for a nap, I see. Mum just popped round the corner so it's just you and me, girls. Fancy a cup of tea?"

"Er – Dad?"

"Yes, Suz?"

"Are your cups of tea anything like your gravy?"

"You cheeky monkey! No I think my tea is rather better than my gravy!"

Kathy giggled. In fact they all giggled when they remembered the gravy that Dad had made when Mum had gone to stay with Granma, gravy so solid that they had had to cut it into slices and drop it onto the plates.

Susan left Kathy and Dad reminiscing.

30

Fear on the Pier and the Old Man

Peter had had some difficulty finding their bottle which someone had mistaken for rubbish and, when Susan joined him on the beach he was using his T-shirt to wipe off the remains of coffee and sticky doughnut which had landed on top of it in the bin.

The photo session had restarted with Miss Lister walking barefoot on the sand and wearing the skimpiest of bikinis. She really *was* beautiful. But Susan didn't wish her mum was a model. She actually liked coming home and having someone ask her what had happened at school, even if it meant telling half-truths or avoiding the truth altogether. It was obvious that Steven's mum wasn't often home at all. No, she wouldn't want that.

"Here, Thuthan. I can't get thith thticky bit off."

"Not to worry. The important thing is that we've got the bottle, not how clean it is. Let's go to the pier as quickly as possible."

It was important for him to promise not to run off again because she knew that she might need someone to grab hold of if her knees went funny. Still, being four years older than her brother, Susan didn't want to appear a sissy.

The first part of the pier was enclosed and Susan had a moment to glance around. The lady in the booth with the prizes was just going for a tea break but everyone else was full of energy and the pier buzzed with excitement as children aimed toy guns at moving ducks, in the hope of getting a token which they could exchange for a prize, men pushed coins eagerly into slot machines, and women tried their hand at formula one racing. However, it was the noise that came from the brightly coloured machines, each one playing a different tune or speaking with robotic voices that really caught Susan's attention.

But it was when she arrived at the far end of the pier that there was a problem.

Peter, who up till then had been just as keen to watch everyone as she, was not about to wait for a sister who was four years older than him, and promptly did exactly what she had hoped he wouldn't. He ran off. The instant they stepped foot on the pier itself, he simply disappeared, leaving her with the bottle and her fear of heights and open spaces.

Suddenly terror decided to keep her company. Whether it was the fear itself or fear of being afraid, Susan froze on the spot as she saw Peter skipping from the left side of the pier to the right to hang over first one rail and then the other.

She knew that she should go and rein Peter in immediately, but she just couldn't seem to make herself walk out onto those planks through the gaps of which she could see the water far below.

"Excuse me, Miss," someone next to her said. "I wonder if you would mind helping me get to that bench over there."

Looking around, she saw a little old man standing next to her, carrying one of those white sticks that blind people use to guide themselves. Susan did not hesitate. Slipping one arm through his, she walked out onto the pier.

"I don't like walking here alone because of the gaps between the planks," he told her. "You see, it's easy to get my stick stuck. But this is one of my favourite spots. In summers past, my wife and I used to spend mornings out here just sitting and having a nice cup of tea. Well, she's gone now, is my dear Dot. But I still love coming here. The sound of the seagulls is so comforting. Somehow it's possible to imagine my Dot sitting beside me. Oh, here we are. My, I have nattered on, haven't I? You are so kind, my dear. Thank you for helping."

Susan bent over as she helped him lower himself down onto the bench, and suddenly realized that she had made it! And it had been so much easier than she had expected. Helping someone else had helped her. Holding the man's arm had given her courage.

As for Peter, he was talking to a boy about his own age who, from the look of the line he was holding, was probably catching crabs. In fact, as she and her companion drew closer, he jerked it back and plop, a crab the size of Susan's palm landed on its back right in front of her, its legs waving madly in the air. Flicking it over with a stick, the boy picked it up and dropped it into his bucket.

She could see that Peter was itching to have a go but just then the owner of the pier walked over to the boy and told him to empty the bucket over the side which, clearly reluctantly, he did. After watching his treasures disappear in the water below he picked up his gear and left the pier.

"Did you thee that?" Peter demanded, running to join Susan. "He'd got a whole bucket-full. He thaid hith mum wath going to cook them for tea."

"Don't go suggesting to our Mum that she prepare crab for us too!" Susan warned him.

"Thpoil thport! When are we going to throw the bottle in?"

"I thought you'd never ask."

"Excuse me," said the old man. "I don't mean to be rude but I do hope you're not throwing rubbish in the sea?"

"Oh, no," Peter said. "Of courth not. We've got a methage in a bottle and we want to thee if anyone findth it and cometh to thee uth in our hotel."

"I see," the old man smiled. "That's different, of course. Well, good luck to both of you and thank you again for your help, Miss."

It had, Susan realized, as he made his way to back down the pier, tapping his way carefully with his white stick, been extraordinarily pleasant to have been able to help him. And then, turning her attention to Peter, she followed him, walking as close to him as she dare, without letting him see that she was scared, to the end of the pier and watched him throw the bottle into the water.

"Look, Thuthan. It'th drifting over to that group of boyth."

Sure enough there were four boys and one girl playing in the water with a basketball. They were making a real din and did not pay the slightest bit of attention to the plastic bottle as it floated between them.

Susan looked at her watch. "We're late for dinner, Pete. We'd better get going otherwise there'll be trouble."

"Can't we thtay and watch who pikth it up?"

"No, it'll be more fun if we don't see. Let's get going!"

Fortunately dinner was being served later than usual since most of the guests staying in the hotel had gone over to have a look at the filming on the beach and so Susan and Peter were not alone in arriving late. Of course, Mum and Dad had been as punctual as ever and were already eating when they planted themselves down on their chairs.

"May we ask where you two got to?"

"We'd rather you didn't!" Susan said. "You see it's a bit of a secret."

"Just so long as it's nothing we should worry about, Susan," Dad said. "I suggest you eat before it gets cold."

The waiter placed a scrumptious looking plate of sausages, mashed potato and thick rich gravy, Gran's favourite, in front of Susan. It didn't take long to polish it off and then came apple pie and vanilla ice-cream.

"How's Kathy?"

"Sleeping and blistering, I'm afraid," Mum answered, "I'm not sure she's going to be up to having the photo taken with Miss Lister."

"Tunky, let's wait and see, shall we?" Dad said. "From what she was telling me she very much wants to be up and about again by then, even if it means going straight back to bed afterwards."

Susan hoped Kathy would be feeling better. She could just imagine Helena and Gemma's expressions in school when she showed them the photo. It would definitely be something worth bragging about, she thought. They would be green with envy.

31

Steven in Trouble

Strangely, the afternoon dragged. With their spot on the beach taken and Kathy unwell, nobody really knew what to do with themselves. It was too hot for Susan to go back outside and so she and Peter found themselves in the games room, chatting to Nanny and occasionally looking through the window to see what was happening.

At about four o'clock, the cameras, stage, lights and chairs were all packed up and the caravans and trailers headed for the pier. People wandered away slowly and an eerie silence descended on the beach. Susan went to ask Mum if she could go over to their spot alone, with her sketch pad.

Permission having been granted, Susan, notebook and pencil in her hand, crossed the road, went down the steps and found a patch of sand that didn't have plastic cups and hamburger wrappers strewn on it. It was, she thought, a real mess for Bucket-chomping Harry to clean up.

Opening her sketch book, Susan realised that she didn't need anybody to tell her that her sketch of the hotel was good. She knew it was. And that was good enough for her on this occasion.

It was the last opportunity she would have to draw it because, if it really *was* converted into flats, she knew it would never look the same as it did today. At least, in having done a sketch, she would have captured something on paper of her Teignmouth holidays.

"Thuthan, Thuthan. Where are you?"

"Down here, Peter."

"Theven'th mum'th ready and Kathy'th up and – Come on!"

She stood up, shook the sand off, picked up her flip flops and walked back to the steps. Just one day left and they would say goodbye forever.

"Here I am," she said when she reached the top of the stairs. "Where is everyone?"

"Over there," and Peter pointed to the steps of the hotel.

For some reason Susan had expected the whole camera crew to be there as well but only Mr. Chris was waiting. He quickly told them where to stand, took several casual shots in quick succession, and then announced that he had finished and that he ought to be hitting the road.

"I'll be back the day after tomorrow, Liz. Make sure you get some rest tomorrow. I need you ready and looking refreshed for the book signing."

"Yes, Chris. I know. I hope you got some good ones today."

"With you, darling, I never fail!" He kissed her on both cheeks, threw his heavy camera bag on the passenger seat of his black Porsche, which was parked on the pavement, got in and pulled away with a screech of burning tyres.

"Well, children, I am going to have a nice long soak in the bath," Steven's mum said. "Hope you enjoyed today."

"Oh, yes, Miss Lister," they chorused. "Thank you for inviting us."

"Mum's signing her book on Saturday. Will you come?" Steven was holding his mum's hand and looking up at her with pride and love written all over his face.

"We have to leave on Saturday, Steven," Susan said, hating the thought.

"The book signing is going to be in the reception hall just after breakfast, isn't it , Mum?"

"We'll try, Steven," his mum replied, though not, thought Susan, sounding terribly convincing.

They all walked into the hotel together, past Mrs. Gerty, up the stairs and to their separate rooms.

"Is tomorrow really our last day?" asked Kathy, her hand on the door knob.

"'Fraid so, Kiff," Susan said. "I do hope you're feeling better. Oh, blast. I forgot to ask Steven where he bought the whimsy he gave you. You go on in. I'll just go and knock on their door just in case he's not at tea."

But at the sound of raised voices, Susan wished that she had not.

"GET THE BLASTED DOOR, WILL YOU AND STOP BLUBBERING LIKE A GIRL."

Steven opened the door an inch and looked embarrassed to see Susan standing there.

"Sorry, Steven," Susan said. "It's just I forgot to ask you something. That little sea horse you gave Kathy? Can you remember where you got it?"

"I was with Mum," he told her. "She'll remember. Let me go and ask her."

"No, Ste...," Susan began, but it was too late. Off he went, leaving the door ajar.

The shouting began again immediately, and although Susan tried hard not to listen, it was impossible not to hear Steven's dad. His voice was strange - slurred somehow - and he was using words that Dad called 'gutter language.'

Why, she asked herself, had she gone back over to Steven's room?

"Mum said to give you this," Steven mumbled, as he cracked the door open. But before he could say anything else someone jerked him back into the room and the door slammed shut. The last thing Susan heard, before running for the shelter of her own room, was Steven crying out in pain.

32

Dad to the Rescue

"Everything alright, Suz?"

Susan shook her head. She couldn't speak. Her mind was in a whirl.

"Susan, come here."

She went to stand by her dad's chair.

"Tell me what's wrong."

"I think Steven's dad just hit him," Susan gasped. "He's saying awful things and shouting and swearing and Steven cried out when his dad pulled him back into the room."

Susan saw the colour drain from her father's face.

"Did you actually see Steven's dad hit him?" he asked her.

Had she, Susan wondered, made a mistake in telling Dad this? Should she have pretended that no one had been there?

"No, but it was obvious. Oh, Dad please stop him."

"Susan, it's not as easy as that," her father said. "I can certainly go and check if things are quieter but I can't go barging in just like that claiming that someone's being beaten."

"Maybe he'll kill him," added Peter helpfully.

"Peter," Mum exclaimed. "I don't think that was necessary. But he does have a point, Mike."

"Dad, please help him," Kathy, who had been silent until now, looked as if she were about to cry. "He's been really nice to us this holiday. We can't sit and do nothing."

"Gosh, I can see I have my whole family ganging up against me," Dad said, looking put upon.

"Darly!"

"All right. All right. I'm going!"

They all waited for what seemed ages before, suddenly, there was a commotion in the corridor with men yelling at each other and doors slamming. Kathy pulled her knees up to her chest, Peter cuddled up to Mum and Susan chewed her thumb nails.

"You were right to push me," were Dad's words when, at long last, he returned, cheeks blazing. "The owner of the hotel was informed and he decided that the police had to be called in. Steven will be fine tonight, his mother is with him. His dad has been taken down to the station.

"When will he come back?"

"That, my darling Suz, is entirely up to the police."

The police! Susan had never expected it to go this far. And all because of her.

33

The Sardine, the Cat and Mrs. Gerty

"I hate to mention it, but it is actually time for tea."

"Oh, Mum, do we have to. "I'm not hungry."

"Thpeak for yourthelf, Thuthan. I'm thtarving."

"You're always starving!"

"Before an argument begins, children, let's get down to the dining room and we can discuss what we're going to do on our penultimate evening."

"Our what?"

"Penultimate, Kathy. It means the last but one. It comes from the Latin for..."

"Dad, please don't mention Latin on holiday!"

"Susan! You, young lady should know what it means."

"The only words I can remember in Latin are puella, puer and agricola – oh yes, and Mensa, mensa, mensam and I don't think I will get very far in life being able to talk about girls, boys, farmers and tables!"

"If we're going to have tea could you two please continue this fascinating conversation over sardines."

"SARDINES? AGAIN? MUM!"

"I thought you all liked sardines?"

"We do Mum. But not five times in two weeks!"

"You should have told me. We could have ordered something different."

At least they were being distracted from worrying about Steven and his father. It was only as they were walking down together to the dining room that Susan realized that she was still clutching the slip of paper that Steven had shoved at her. She opened it and read the delicate, perfect calligraphy.

"Go to the small antique shop, opposite the post office – ask Mr Price to show you his Whimsey collection – Tell him Miss Lister sent you."

The signature was as elegant as the lady who had written it. Susan popped the paper into her pocket and followed the others in for tea.

"What is better?"
Said the fish
As he lay on the plate.
"To be out in the sea
Or out on a date?"

Said the crab
to the fish
"It is better by far
To be sardine in here
Than out there in the dark"

But the boy
to the crab
had a different view
"I'd prefer you alive
Than in my..."

"PETER! I don't think we need the next word, Thank you very much."

"But Mum, it rhymeth"

"I'm well aware of that! But we are just about to eat."

Giggles rippled round the table and Susan waited for Dad's "enough is enough" but it didn't come. Peter's giggles got louder but when he tried to recite the sardine poem again, he was warned by a kick under the table from Susan that he was pushing his luck.

There followed a minute or two during which all that could be heard was the clinking of forks and knives on porcelain. And then the ultimate happened.

Peter spied Gerty's cat who was plodding his way through the dining room looking from side to side and occasionally licking his lips. Picking up one of his sardines, he tossed it to Paddy. The cat jumped to catch it, but being as heavy as he was, only managed to lift his two front paws off the ground, with the result that the sardine flew over his head and landed smack, bang, wallop on Mrs. Gerty's shoe. She shrieked and Paddy pounced. Snapping up his prize, he retreated under the nearest table, which happened to be the Thomas family's! And Mrs. Gerty, with her usual promptitude added two and two together and turned to confront them.

"IN ALL MY BORN DAYS I HAVE NOT SEEN SUCH IMPUDENCE, SUCH BAD BEHAVIOUR, SUCH LACK OF MANNERS!" she declared. "YOU REALLY DO NEED TO KEEP YOUR CHILDREN UNDER CONTROL."

"And it might be advisable for you to keep your temper under control." Dad spoke with the full force of a headmaster's authority. Mrs. Gerty flushed an even deeper red when the proprietor came in from the kitchen.

"Is everything in order?" he asked, frowning. "I thought I heard someone shouting."

And then, seeing Dad, he extended his hand.

"It's nothing, really," Mrs. Gerty assured him. "Just some children and their – pranks. I'm sure they didn't mean any harm."

"Mrs. Gerty, if I may have a word." Mr. James opened his arm to show her the way out but she was in no mood to be escorted anywhere. Instead she stomped out leaving a very happy cat rubbing Peter's legs in the hope he might get another treat.

"Thorry, Dad!"

"That's my boy. Just think twice next time and learn to be rather more observant."

Mr. James collared Dad as they were returning to their room.

"I do apologize for Mrs. Gerty. She's had a hard time of it lately, what with her brother in hospital and being out of a job in a month or two. I'm afraid she's taking all of it rather badly."

Susan only just managed to keep her mouth shut. She would love to have asked him why it was, then, that

Mrs. Gerty had been so moody the previous year and the year before that.

"I understand. I fear my children's exuberance hasn't made the last couple of weeks any easier." Susan heard her father say.

"No, I'm sure it hasn't, but even I must admit I chuckled when I heard of the mouse incident and the bosom note."

Susan kept her eyes fixed to a dirty spot on the floor. Now would not be a good moment to look at her Dad.

"The what?"

"I see you missed the fun. It's a – hmm – it's nothing really."

"I see!" Dad said, but from the puzzled tone of his voice, Susan realised he clearly did not see at all.

"Well, I wish you a pleasant evening. Your penultimate, if I'm not mistaken?"

"If I don't see you all tomorrow to say goodbye, I'd like to say what a pleasure it has been to have such faithful guests over all these years. I do hope you will remember your stays with fondness."

It was a formal response, but Susan could sense real feeling behind the words. How difficult it must be, she thought, to say goodbye to people you would never see again. And as Dad said that they were taking with them many wonderful memories of Teignmouth, tears came to her eyes.

And then he returned to the kitchen, leaving Mum and Dad facing their children, their arms folded across their chests, frown marks getting deeper and deeper by the minute.

Susan knew they were waiting for an explanation, but it wasn't going to come from her. Kathy and Peter clearly had the same thought.

The moment passed. Arms dropped to sides, frown marks relaxed and then, thankfully, the moment passed, probably, Susan realised, because her parents wanted their last evening to be a pleasant one, particularly after the Steven episode. So it was that Dad suggested a walk on the promenade and ice-cream for all.

34

The Bottle Children Appear

It was a nice, warm evening, just perfect for sitting on a bench. Marigolds in the flowerbeds behind them gave off a heady fragrance which came and went with the breeze from the sea.

The colours of the freshly painted hotels behind them, the grass on the hills, the sea itself, all the hues were richer, deeper in the evening sunlight. The family stayed together, Peter tempting the seagulls every now and again with pieces of ice cream cone, until the lanterns came on and the string of coloured lights between each lamp post began to glow. It was one of those rare, magic moments where everything is just perfect.

But, when darkness finally descended, Mum and Dad rose. "They'll be closing the front door soon and it wouldn't do much good to be shut out tonight especially as it's Mrs. Gerty's task to open the door for latecomers!" Dad observed.

They arrived just as that formidable lady was putting the key in the lock. Susan noticed that she didn't look at them when they said, "Good evening."

"Phew! That was close!"

"You're telling me," Mum replied. "Children, straight up, undressed and into bed, please. Dad and I will just see if the dining room is still open for a quick cup of tea. We'll be up in a while."

Susan slipped her arm through Kathy's who winced, "Ow. Don't touch me there!"

"Sorry, Kiff. You're still not feeling very well, are you?"

"I'm just sort of woozy. I can't wait to get back to my own bed."

"You actually want to go home?"

"Yes. Don't you?"

Susan didn't answer. The hotel was shutting, Lee had gone back to California, There wasn't anything to keep her here and yet – No, she didn't want to go home.

"There's one more day," she said. "And I intend to make the most of it!"

As they were getting into bed, Susan opened the window to let in some fresh air and suddenly remembered the message in the bottle. Because, there standing on the other side of the road, under the lamp post, holding the bottle in her hand was a girl with shoulder length blond hair, dressed in a T-shirt and jeans and looking about her in every direction, as though she were waiting for someone.

Next to her was a tall, lanky boy, his hands shoved in his pockets.

"Kathy, Peter," Susan hissed. "Quick! Look!"

Peter came running with Kathy right behind him.

"Let'th go and thee them. I'll put my troutherth back on."

"We can't. Gerty's locked the door, remember!"

"Oh, Gordon Bennett!"

It was a jolly good thing that the children couldn't get out because, at that very moment, a policeman came along the promenade and took the bottle from the girl. Then, after speaking to someone on his walky-talky, marched them back in the direction of the pier.

"That boy wath one of the group thwimming near the pier earlier," Peter said.

"In that case," Susan said, hoping he was right, "we can try and find them on the beach tomorrow."

Just then Mum and Dad opened the door.

"I thought we said straight to bed. Now!" Mum said. "We've got a lot of packing to do tomorrow. Didn't you say the book-signing was in the morning, Susan?"

"It's on Saturday," Susan told her, wishing her Mum had not reminded her of how little time they had left.

"Right, sleep tight, all of you! Darly, close the window, will you?"

Susan forced herself to stay awake till everyone was breathing regularly, all the time trying to remember what

225

Lee looked like. If she could picture him before nodding off maybe they would spend the night sharing hopes and dreams again. But she couldn't get a clear picture and fell asleep thinking of messages in bottles, flying sardines and crabs instead.

35

Miss Lister's Invitation

Peter jumping on them in the morning was becoming routine and today was no exception.

"Hi guyth! Bucket-chomping Harry'th cleaning our beach for us!"

"Would you mind getting off my foot, brother dear!" Susan said, stretching and yawning.

"But of courth! Better?"

"Much. Who's that Mr. Harry's got with him in the tractor?"

"I dunno, can't thee. Hey, maybe it'th hith graddaughter. What'th her name?"

"Anna, I think."

"He wanted her to thee our boat."

"Bit late for that. Gosh, that was ages ago! Well, we won't have time to build a new one today, that's for sure. What time is it?"

"Half patht nine! Hang your knickerth on the line. When the politheman comes along..."

"What do you think the policeman did with those two kids last night?" Susan whispered.

"Shut them in prithon with Thteven'th dad?"

"Why do I ever try to have a sensible conversation with you?"

"'Coth I'm tho intelligent!"

"What are you two talking about? Move over Susan, my feet are cold."

Kathy pulled her sister's covers gently over her peeling legs.

"You're looking more perky!" Susan said.

"Can I pull the thkin off your nothe?" Peter added.

"NO, you can't." Kathy smacked Peter's hand as he lifted it to help a big piece of peeling skin come free. "You should see my bed, Susan. It's like someone's emptied a bucket of dandruff all over it. I know the doctor said I can't pull at it. But I can't stop it rubbing itself off."

"Yuk! I must say you're beginning to look like a blotchy sheep that's been badly sheared," Susan said, peering under her sheet. "It'll be more fun if you're feeling better. We want to go and try and find that girl and boy with the bottle."

"What are you three scheming this time?" Dad said sleepily. "Nothing that involves Mrs. Gerty, I hope?"

"No way. We're not that stupid!" Susan assured him.

"I'm glad to hear it! Tunky, time to stir."

"No, I'm staying here!"

"I think she needs some help, kids!"

"Here we come! I'll tickle her toeth."

"I'll grab the covers and Kathy, why don't you grab her glass of water?"

"Stop it! Peter! – oh – eh – aa – don't! OK! I'm up. I'm up!"

Steven and his mum were already eating breakfast when they arrived. Both looked up and smiled and Susan saw Miss Lister mouth "Thank you" to Dad as they passed. She was relieved to see that they both looked happy, though it was obvious that Steven's cheek was bruised.

On her way out of the dining room, Miss Lister stopped to speak to Mum who was munching on her toast and apricot jam. Susan couldn't hear what she said, but she saw Mum smile and nod her head.

"Susan, can you be ready in ten minutes?" she said when Steven's mother had left the dining room.

"It depends on what for!" Susan replied cautiously.

Miss Lister needs to pop along the promenade and she's offered to escort you to Mr. Price's – the antique dealer. It didn't make much sense to me but when she said "Whimsey" I agreed. I take it you know what she's talking about?"

"Really?"

"Why would I make something like that up? Of course, it's really."

"Wow. Me with Miss Lister! Oh, is Steven going too?"

"No, that was part of the bargain. She's asked if he could spend the morning with us. She has a couple of things that she urgently has to take care of. She asked you to knock at number 11 when you are ready. And remember..."

But Mum was talking to thin air. Susan had left already, her cup of tea half drunk and her prunes untouched.

36

Susan Transformed

"What am I going to wear? What am I going to wear?"

Susan had had the forethought to grab the key from Dad as she raced from the table, and now, as she tossed her clothes on the bed, she saw what a mess they were. Creased, colours not matching, unfashionable and old. And her hair! What a wreck!

Just then there was a tap at the door and Miss Lister popped in.

"I thought you might be having this problem," she said cheerfully. "Let's see what we've got here. She picked up a light cream V-necked T-shirt with buttons down the front and an old pair of brown shorts.

"Now show me what shoes you've got," she added.

Susan bent down and pulled a pair of brown sandals from under the bed."

"Follow me," she said , tucking the bundle of clothes under her arm.

Her room was larger than Susan's and through an open door, she could see that there was an en suite bathroom. There was another door on the opposite wall and from the other side there was the sound of gunshot and loud screeching music which indicated to Susan that Steven had his own bedroom.

"Don't worry," his mother assured her. "Steven knows he's not to disturb us. Now slip this on."

In seconds Susan had changed into her new outfit, strangely unembarrassed at being seen almost naked by someone she didn't know.

"Now let me try something." Steven's mum opened the top drawer of her bedside table and took out a silk scarf in all shades of pink, cream and brown. Slipping it around Susan's shoulders, she deftly tied it at the front and stood back to take a look.

"Come and stand over here," she said opening the door of her wardrobe to display a long mirror in which Susan found herself reflected. Amazingly enough, just the scarf itself had transformed her outfit and she actually thought she looked quite pretty. But she was not prepared for what happened next. Miss Lister removed the bobble from Susan's hair and with her own brush lifted and fluffed and fiddled and 'umm-ed' and 'aah-ed' until at last she stood aside and Susan gasped. Never would she have believed it possible. She was staring at a beautiful young lady who moved as she did and looked just as surprised as she did at the transformation.

"I always longed for a daughter," Steven's mum said. "Don't get me wrong. Not instead of Steven. My, my! No! But as a sister for him. You are a beautiful young lady, Susan. Sorry I barged in on you like I did but I couldn't resist and I was sure you wouldn't mind. You're not cross, are you?"

"Oh, no! It's just – how did you do it? How..."

"All you need to do is learn a few tricks and the rest is just hard work."

Miss Lister sounded tired. She turned her head away and Susan could swear that she saw her wipe away a tear.

"Let me just put some lipstick on and we'll be off," she said. "I told your mum I'd have you back by eleven-thirty, which gives us plenty of time to visit Mr. Price's. Steven? Ready!" There was no answer. "Steven, come on love. I need to lock up." She opened the door and Steven looked up from the bed. He was watching a film on his laptop, but didn't seem too unhappy at being interrupted.

"I'll just switch my laptop off," he said and then he caught sight of Susan.

"Wow, Susan! Is that you? Gosh! Mum, what did you do? She looks incredible!"

"She's an attractive girl who's just discovered how pretty she really is," his mother told him. "It would be the same with you, too if you learned to take a bit more care of yourself and had your hair cut every once in a while!"

"Come off it, Mum. You always say there's more to life than looks."

"Well, for today let's just pretend I was joking!"

"Susan, I hope you have not you been imposing on Miss Lister?" was all Dad could say when he saw his gorgeous daughter.

"Now, now, Mr. Thomas. Let her have some fun. She's my guest for the morning and we've been experimenting."

"Before you say anything, Susan," said Miss Lister as they walked out in the sunshine, "He's your dad and it's obvious he loves you. Be grateful for that. I have a feeling he'd like to hold on to you forever. But it is fine for you to grow up and spread your wings, you know."

Susan was on cloud nine, aware that everyone on the promenade was turning to look at them.

As they passed the pier a group of lads turned and wolf-whistled and called out to her, but she had to guess what they were saying because it wasn't in English. Among the group was the boy who had been outside her window the previous night. He looked at her, as well, and then, clearly embarrassed, looked away quickly.

Had she been alone, Susan would probably have stopped and spoken to him. After all, he and his friends had found the bottle. But that could come later, she told herself. Right now Steven's mother was taking her somewhere, and more than anything, she wondered why.

37

The Antique Shop

Susan had never noticed the antique shop. Maybe it was because it was set back a little from the path and the windows were dark. Certainly there was nothing inviting about it. The wood had been stained black and she supposed the lettering painted above the grimy window panes had once been gold. But the colour had faded, as had half the name. But, oh, what a contrast the interior was, the small shop filled to overflowing with all sorts of trinkets, as well as brass horse shoes, glass lamps, cabinets of silver cutlery and even an old book case full of antique cars, and a display case with little silver pencil sharpeners. There was the smell of polish and everything shone.

A ship's bell rang as the heavy door opened and an old man who looked vaguely familiar appeared from the back, wiping his hands in his dirty apron. He stooped a little and wore dark glasses.

"Liz, is that you?" he exclaimed. "You just caught me. I was just about to go and take my morning walk on the pier." And guiding himself by holding onto the counter, he bent to kiss Miss. Lister's hand.

"Well, if it isn't my young helper!" he said when he saw Susan. "Hello again, my dear."

Now Susan knew where she'd seen him before. He was the gentleman she'd helped on the pier.

"Good morning, Sir."

"Oh, no sirs for me," he told her. "I'm Mr. Price to my neighbours and Cliff to my friends. Now Liz, what can I do for you today?"

"I was just telling Susan," Steven's mother began.

"What a lovely name!"

"Yes, she's a lovely girl. I was hoping you might show her your collection of Whimsies. She hasn't been able to find any in Teignmouth this year and a little bird told me she buys one each year."

"Do you indeed? Well, you've certainly come to the right place. Follow me!"

Susan watched as Mr. Price felt his way down a narrow corridor which was lined with more shelves, each overflowing with yet more antiques.

"He's blind, though you wouldn't know it," Miss. Lister said in a low voice. "He once told me he knows where every item is in his shop and can tell what people have been looking at because they put things down in the wrong place."

"Liz, you don't have to whisper!" Mr. Price said. "I don't mind you telling Susan how an old man copes in an antique shop. But please remember to add that I have been here for sixty-two years. Someone will put me on the shelf one day because they'll mistake me for one of the antiques! Right. In here."

The old wooden door creaked as he pushed it and led the way into a room that was no larger than the box room in Susan's grandparent's house. But rather than boxes and a fold-up bed this room had shadow boxes on every wall and in each compartment there was a whimsy. Susan did a quick calculation. One shadow box held about fifty ornaments and there must have been going on for twenty shadow boxes.

"What do you think, my dear?" the old man said.

Susan was speechless. She had been excited with her eleven ornaments, but over one thousand? Granted, she could see many doubles and she spotted one shadow box which was devoted to horses, many of which were identical. But still!

"This has to be my favourite," he said, and pulling out a small step ladder he used his fingers to feel along the wall. He stopped, stood on the second step, reached up and ran his hand along the bottom edge of a very old shadow box.

"Here, he is," he said and gently, between finger and thumb, he brought down a little brown spaniel.

"It's beautiful. Where did you buy it?"

"My mother gave it to me when I was about your age. It was my very first and reminded me of my very own spaniel, Jem. I began to collect dogs after that and you can tell my fascination didn't stop when I had completed my first set."

Instead of handing his treasure to Susan to hold he placed it gently back in its spot before climbing down and pushing the ladder back under a work bench. As they approached the door, he paused under the smallest display box which contained just figurines, each one a little lady, no bigger than Susan's thumb, dressed in long, full skirts.

"That is the "My Fair Lady" collection," Mr. Price said with a smile, "I gave them to *my* fair lady when I asked for her hand in marriage. She promised she would love me, and my ornaments to the end. And, my word, she did!"

"They are so pretty."

Mr. Price came to where Susan was standing and took her right hand in both of his. "Come with me, my angel. I have one more thing to show you."

Still holding her hand he led her back to his work table which had one long drawer running the length of its scratched surface.

"Go on," he said. "Open it."

Susan had to pull quite hard, and on several occasions, the drawer got stuck, but with some persuading, she managed to tug it open.

Inside, lying on pieces of tissue paper, yellow with age, were about twenty Whimseys. She had seen replicas of most of them on the wall but the one in particular that caught her eye was a miniature girl holding a balloon close to her chest. It was not exactly the same as the girl she'd seen through the window because this child was standing and smiling.

"I'd like you to have one," Mr Price said. It was, she thought, as though he had read her mind. "I haven't had a moment to put up another shadow box and to tell you the truth it would be difficult to find wall space to hang it. But I do so hate them being shut in a drawer."

"Are you sure?" Susan asked quietly.

"Mr. Price doesn't make light of his words, Susan," she heard Miss Lister say quietly.

It was with an overwhelming sense of wonderment that Susan reached into the drawer and lifted out the little girl. Handing it to Mr. Price, she saw his smile as he caressed it.

"Ah! Nina, Josanya! Not a Whimsey, I'm afraid. You'll notice it doesn't have "Wade©" engraved on the base, but she is very sweet. I hope you'll give her a good home. She deserves it, does Josanya. But I can't send you home without a genuine Whimsey. If you like Josanya you'll like this one too." And he felt in the drawer one more time until he found another girl. It was a beautiful Whimsey Little Bo Peep.

Susan was hoping he might tell her something about when he had acquired these two ornaments but he didn't. Instead he reached up to a shelf above the table, took down a little cardboard box and two small squares of fresh tissue paper, wrapped the two girls separately, placed them into the box, shut the lid and put the box into Susan's hand, holding her hand in his one more time before sighing and straightening up as much as he could.

"Thank you, Cliff," said Miss Lister, holding the door open for Susan.

"You are more than welcome. Both of you."

Before they turned to walk out of the box room Susan reached over and kissed Mr. Price on his cheek.

"Thank you ever so much, Mr. Price. I promise I will look after them."

"Yes, I know you will," he told her.

"Susan, it's ten past eleven," Miss Lister said. "Your mum and dad will be looking for us soon. Thank you again, Cliff. I should be back in a day or two to say goodbye before Steven and I leave."

"Everything sorted out?"

"Almost. I have a meeting in an hour which should conclude matters."

"Well, my dear ladies. Enjoy the rest of the day. They've forecast another hot one."

"Goodbye, Mr. Price."

"Goodbye, Susan. I look forward to seeing you again soon. Hmmm. You know what I mean!"

They left the antique shop and walked swiftly back into the square.

"I'll have to leave you here, I'm afraid," Miss. Lister said when they arrived at the fountain. "I'm due somewhere else in a little while. Please tell Steven I'll pick him up for dinner. And Susan, in some ways this is going to be a hard day for me, but it has been a delight for me to see the twinkle in your eye."

38

Pen-pals

Susan watched as Steven's mother walked away across the Triangles, and thought with pleasure about the morning, as well as the wonderful week. And now there was just one afternoon to go!

With ten minutes left before she had to be back at the hotel, Susan sat down on the wall just outside the pier entrance where she'd first seen Lee and took a peek in her little box. She wouldn't be going home without a Whimsey after all.

As she was about to stand up, a girl sat down just a meter away from her and buried her nose in a book. Susan was certain that it was the girl she'd seen outside her window with their bottle, but when she asked her about it, it was clear from the girl's tentative response that English was not her native language. And so Susan rested the box on her lap and proceeded to mime what a bottle was, pretending to screw and unscrew the lid.

"Oh, Yes. Bottle. I found and my friend."

She pointed to a group of boys huddled on the beach just beyond the pier, who were passing a mobile phone back and forth and laughing raucously, now and then pausing to urge on another boy with a head of tight curls who was busy digging a hole in the sand. It was, Susan realised, the same group who had whistled at her that morning.

"My name's Susan."

"I'm Justine," the girl told her. "I'm from Poland. And you?"

"Oh, I'm English," Susan said. "Why are you in Teignmouth?"

"We are in Teignmouth only three days. Sunday we back to Taunton for English school."

"Oh, I see. How old are you?"

"I'm twelve and the boys they are thirteen. Maybe you give me your e-mail and we can write. You know-friends with pen?"

"You mean pen-pals? I haven't got a computer but I can give you my snail mail address."

"Snail mail?"

"Sorry. Postal address? Letters? Stamps? Post office?"

Susan began miming the writing of a letter. It was like playing charades, but she could see that the girl still didn't understand her.

Going to the nearby ice-cream booth, she asked for two paper napkins on which she wrote her name and address while the Polish girl wrote her e-mail address on the other. Susan was puzzled by some of the letters and had to ask her to write it again in capitals just to make sure.

"Maybe I can use the school computer," she said. "Gosh, I must go. My mum is waiting. Are you going to be here in the afternoon?"

"Sorry?"

"Later? Three o'clock? Here?" she explained, again tapping her watch, holding up three fingers and pointing to the beach.

Susan was relieved to see Justine nod and indicate that her friends would be there too. She would have hated to miss the opportunity to meet such an interesting group of boys and had a strange feeling that there was an adventure waiting for her.

39

Time to Pack

"We're here, Thuthan," Peter shouted.

The rest of the family was on the beach with Steven and a little blond girl. The children were playing Piggy in the Middle, throwing a ball high over Steven's head. As Susan watched, he raced to get it, skidding purposefully on the sand and, in the process, colliding with Peter. They both landed clumsily in a heap amidst roars of laughter and yells of "I've got it" and "No, you haven't". Susan sat herself down on the edge of the towel between Mum and Dad, and taking the figurine of Josanya from the paper wrapping, held it out from them to see.

"Oh, that *is* pretty!" Mum exclaimed. "How much did it cost?"

"Nothing. Mr. Price gave it to me. And this one too," she said, bringing out Little Bo Peep.

"That was kind of him. Has Miss Lister let you keep the scarf, too?"

Susan put her hand up to her neck.

"No, I forgot I was still wearing it. I'll return it later. She said she'll be back in time to pick Steven up for dinner. I think they're going out somewhere."

Kathy plonked herself at Susan's feet sending a shower of sand over everyone.

"Watch out, Kathy," said Susan hurriedly hiding her ornaments.

"What is it? Show me."

"I'll show you back at the hotel later. Dad, can I have the key so that I can pack this box? I don't want it getting broken."

"Yes, my little model. Here, catch!" and he flipped the key to Susan. It went straight through her open fingers landing beside her on the towel.

"Hmmm," he said. "I can see you need some catching practise. Fancy a game of cricket after dinner?"

"Actually, Dad I met a girl from Poland on the promenade as I was walking back and I told her I'd try and meet her at about three. She's given me her e-mail address and we're going to write to each other."

"Interesting to see how you'll manage that since you don't have a computer."

"I thought I'd see if our I.T. teacher will let me use the school one during lunch time."

"Can I come with you later?" asked Kathy attempting to wink but only managing a blink.

"I thought you had a new friend?" Susan said, glancing over to where the boys were teasing the little girl playfully and hoping that she might be able to meet the bottle children without her brother and sister tagging along.

"Oh, yes. That's Anna. She's eight. She's Mr. Harry's granddaughter. He brought her here specially to meet us. I'm sure he won't mind if she comes too. She's got a packed lunch with her and he said she could have till five o'clock. Imagine she's going to ride all the way home in the tractor!"

"Kathy, are you playing or not? yelled Peter impatiently.

"Coming!" and she went back to join in a new game of tug of war with a towel.

"I won't be long." Susan stood up and rubbed the sand off her shorts.

"Do be careful, Susan," her mother protested. "I got a face full of sand just then. And do you think you could do something about your clothes when you go up to the room. You did leave them all in rather a mess. Why don't you spend a few minutes packing? At least then you'll have the whole afternoon free to do what you want."

Packing was the last thing Susan wanted to do but, hoping that her Mum would be as good as her word, she managed to sort out her various mismatched outfits in record timing and gulped down her dinner, asking for permission to leave the table before her brother and sister had even started their dessert, and dashing out of the hotel before she heard the word 'no'.

40

The Hole

Susan found Justine where she had left her earlier, still reading her book. Only this time there were two girls with her, both with waist-length hair. They were talking very fast and Susan thought it sounded like a lot of "s"-es, "sh"-s and "z"s all joined together in long unintelligible sentences. Poor Justine had to keep looking up and answering questions which were met by loud, uncontrollable guffaws from the darker of the two, she seemed so troubled at being constantly interrupted that Susan hesitated before joining her, relieved to find that her new friend, who introduced her to Victoria and Isa, seemed genuinely glad to see her.

"Hi!" replied the one Justine had pointed to as being Victoria. Isa nodded and looked down. She appeared really shy.

"Justine tell us about the bottle. She's lucky she has pen-pal. Maybe we can write too? It is OK?"

"Yes, sure. Maybe I could ask my two best friends Helena and Gemma if they want to write too! It'll be fun."

"And maybe boys? You have boys?"

"That's more difficult. I go to an all-girls school."

"Girl school?"

"Yes. No boys."

"Ah. Catholic school. Yes?"

"No. Oh, it's difficult to explain. In my town there's one school for girls and one for boys and one for girls and boys mixed."

Susan saw that Justine seemed relieved when the boys called out to them.

The girls jumped up quickly and dashed down to the beach, but Justine stayed put.

"Do you think everything is okay?" Susan asker her.

"Probably, Yes. They're crazy."

"Is that boy still digging that hole?"

"Hole? Ah – hole! Yes, he has digged two hours."

Susan desperately wanted to correct Justina's grammar but was afraid that, if she did, she might embarrass her. It was probably better to let her language teacher point out her mistakes.

Just then Isa, Victoria and two of the boys rushed past them, calling out something that Justine said meant that they had to go back to the hotel. There were still three boys left on the beach, the curly-haired boy up to his neck in a deep hole, the "bottle" boy and one other.

"Do you think you should warn them?"

"Warn them?"

"Tell them? Rain?" said Susan, pointing to a big black cloud that was moving menacingly across the sky.

"No. They get wet! Ha, ha!"

"Drenched more like."

Susan turned to watch the boys. She had already decided there was no point running back to the hotel. She would shelter under the pier entrance if needs be and perhaps Justine would do the same. She supposed that it was strange that she would want to spend her last afternoon with someone she had just met, but Justine had found the bottle after all, and that was a tie between them. Besides, the possibility of corresponding with someone from another country intrigued her.

All of a sudden the black cloud moved in front of the sun and Susan shivered.

It was like night in the middle of the day and a blustery winter's day in the middle of the summer. A wind picked up and the sand on the beach was caught up in flurries like in a snow storm. Susan could see the tractor getting closer but his engine was drowned out by the plaintive cries of the seagulls.

But it wasn't only the engine that was drowned in the wind and the seagulls' screams but the shrieks for help from the two boys on the beach. Turning, Susan saw their arms waving frantically, and then she saw the reason why. The sand around the hole that the boy had dug was sliding into the hole itself. Like a scaled down mountain avalanche playing out in slow motion, she saw the sand gradually cover the boy. The look of panic and horror was engraved on his face as he disappeared from sight.

When Susan saw only the hand left above the sand, she was stirred into action. It was the view through the window. In every detail.

She raced down the steps, taking two at a time, shouting "Police. Call the police."

"I've got it," Susan heard a man say, and turning to see him taking out his mobile, she began to run, waving Mr. Harry toward her with both arms.

Climbing aboard the tractor she managed to gasp out an explanation of what was happening. Telling her to jump down, Mr. Harry spun the machine around almost on the spot.

Releasing a bucket arm which was pinned up against the side of the tractor he went to work to create a channel behind the now non-existent hole, in the hope that the sand would continue to slide. At first nothing happened, but with the help of the boys and Susan who were now digging madly with their hands, they managed to clear his arm. And when they were joined by two men, they were soon able to clear his face and then his chest by which time the fire brigade had arrived.

The two firemen who dashed to the scene pulled Susan and the other diggers away, passing them to two ambulance men who had arrived at the scene at the same moment.

Susan found it impossible to sit at a distance and just watch but she was ordered not to move and there was nothing for it but to hope that what they had been able to do would be enough. She didn't know how long she sat on the step at the back of the ambulance. It felt like forever.

The black cloud passed overhead, still threatening rain, as Justine stood with the other girls, all of them crying while the boys were expressionless and still.

She looked back to the unhappy scene. Mr. Harry had driven his tractor to a safe distance and was climbing down, wiping his brow and walking over to the policemen who were now keeping bystanders away. He said something to them and then headed in Susan's direction.

There were so many firemen and ambulance men around the gaping hole that it was impossible to see what was going on. When Mr. Harry got to the ambulance, he sat down next to Susan and put his arm round her.

"That was very quick thinking, lass," he said as she rested her head on his chest.

"Is he – is he going to be okay?" Susan asked.

"He's unconscious. They're going to take him to the hospital and they say the next few hours will be crucial. But if it hadn't been for you, the hospital wouldn't be necessary at all."

A medic appeared and, crouching down spoke soothingly to Susan. Only when he took her hand did she realise that she was shaking.

"I want you just to sit here for awhile and I'll get you a warm cup of tea," he said. "Good job! You too, sir. You too!"

When he returned with two steaming cups of strong tea, Susan found that she was simply grateful for something to hold on to. She had taken only a few sips when a policeman strode over to them with a notepad open.

"I'm sorry, but I have to ask you a few questions, Miss," he said. "Did you know the lad?"

"No. Only one of his friends. She found the message in our bottle."

"Right," he said, looking sideways at Mr. Harry with a puzzled expression. "Can you tell me where this friend might be?"

"Yes, she's standing over there – the one holding the book," Susan told him, pointing to Justine who was standing behind a yellow tape that had been put in place to stop curious tourists getting too close. "She's from Poland. She and her friends are her for a language camp."

"Thank you Miss," the policeman said. "That'll be all for now although I may have some more questions later." And then turning to Mr. Harry, "Will you stay with her, sir. I don't want her to be alone while we try to locate her parents."

"They'll be easy to find," the tractor driver told him. "They're looking after my granddaughter at the last hotel at the East Cliff end of the promenade. Just ask for the Thomas family."

"Thank you. I will get someone down there right away."

But it wasn't necessary. It must have been close to four o'clock because Mum and Dad, Kathy, Peter and Anna arrived at exactly that moment, their expressions changing from alarm to relief as they saw Susan safe. When her dad tried to get under the yellow tape only to be pushed back by an impatient officer, Susan called out to him and the same officer lifted the tape for him to pass. Oh, she was relieved it was Dad coming over not Mum. He would just hold her. He wouldn't ask her one hundred questions about 'what' and 'why' and 'how'. And she was right. No words passed between them as he wrapped his arms around her.

But, safe as he made her feel, Susan's thoughts were still with the curly haired boy, whose name she realized she didn't even know.

She watched, wide eyed, as the stretcher was lifted into the ambulance and two doctors climbed in. The doors were shut, flashing lights switched on and the ambulance made its way slowly off the beach. It wasn't until it reached the promenade that the wailing sirens were turned on and the whole nightmare became harsh reality.

Susan looked up at her dad and began to weep.

41

Mrs. Gerty's Secret

"Fancy a ride back to the hotel on my tractor, lass?"

Susan nodded. She didn't think her legs would actually manage to walk even the short distance between the pier and the hotel. She was surprised when Mr. Harry told her father that he hoped it was all right if he took Susan back on Bucket-Chomping Harry.

"Anna told me your name," he explained, helping her up beside him.

"I'll go ahead and buy ice-creams for everyone and head back too," Dad said. "We'll keep Anna for you, if that'll help?"

"Yes, please. I've been asked to go down to the station to give a full report so it might take a while."

"I think Anna can cope. She's a lovely little girl."

"She seems to have taken a shine to your Peter," Mr. Harry said.

"Most people do! He's very outgoing is our Pete. Do you want me to run you down to the station in the car?"

"Heavens , No. It's only a five minute walk from the hotel. I'll have a word with Nanny Helen. She and I go back a long way. She'll take good care of your girl till you get there. Here we go, Susan."

Susan was so relieved not to have to face the probability of having to listen to Peter make up a poem about what had happened, and she certainly didn't fancy pats on the back or concerned gazes from thankful onlookers. She just wanted to get off the beach. But she had forgotten about the sort of greeting she might expect to get from Mrs. Gerty who bellowed, "WHAT HAVE YOU BEEN UP TO NOW? WE'VE HAD THE POLICE HERE ASKING FOR YOUR PARENTS."

Mr. Harry dealt with Mrs. Gerty firmly and with amazing effect.

"We need two cups of sweet tea and a piece of your best cake. This child may just have saved someone's life and the last thing she needs right now is a bitter old woman pointing a self-righteous finger at her and telling her to behave."

"I'm sorry, Mr. Harry. I didn't..."

"No. You usually don't. Maybe it's time you did!"

Susan hadn't seen Mrs. Gerty put in her place quite like that before. It was an uncomfortable moment.

'I feel sorry for the old biddy, really," Mr. Harry said when she had gone. "She has never had many friends has Mrs. Gerty. But she could do with lightening up."

Mrs. Gerty returned with a pot of tea and a plate of mouth-watering goodies and suggested they sit in her room down the hall. The room was cold and dark and Mrs. Gerty had to switch a light on so that they could find their way to a chair. When she offered the cakes round, Susan wanted to say no. How could she eat cake when a boy was lying in the hospital?

"Try one, lass," Mr. Harry urged her. "Eating one cake won't affect the lad's life in any way."

She helped herself to her favourite chocolate gateaux and was glad she had.

Mrs. Gerty poured tea for them and stirred the coals in the grate to encourage the fire back to life. Then she sat down opposite and observed them while they ate.

"Right, Mrs. Gerty," Mr. Harry said, finishing his cake. "Is Helen in?"

"It's her afternoon off." Susan had never heard Mrs. Gerty sounding so subdued.

"In that case, I'm leaving Susan here with you until her dad comes." And then, when Susan glanced at Mr. Harry in dismay, "You'll be fine. Won't she, Mrs. Gerty? I'll see you later, Lass. We made a good team today, you and I!"

"I'm sorry I shouted at you like I did." said Mrs. Gerty putting Mr. Harry's cup and saucer back on the tray. "My temper has had me in trouble before and I am old enough to know better. Do you want to tell me what happened today?"

Susan did not and yet, at the same time she did. "I don't know," she said. "It was horrible. There was sand everywhere and seagulls. One minute the boy was there and the next..." Susan caught her breath... "he was gone. His hole just filled in and he was gone."

"What, you mean he fell in a hole?"

"No, he was digging one and it all caved in."

"I've said for years that there should be signs up telling young people not to dig. It was an accident waiting to happen. I gather it was you that informed the police?"

"No, I was digging. We managed to get his face out. His lips were blue. Oh, it was awful."

"You were actually digging?"

"Yes. Me and two of his friends – and Mr. Harry."

"I see. And the boy now?"

"We don't know. They said something about the first few hours being crucial."

"So there's still hope, then?"

"I guess so."

"So we'll remain hopeful." There was a long pause before Mrs. Gerty continued gravely. "There was no hope for my son. He died on a beach in Normandy, you know."

"I didn't know you were married!"

"It was a long time ago," Mrs. Gerty explained. "My husband passed away when Jeremy was just six years old so he didn't have to receive the telegram with news of our son's death. Here's a picture. He looks grand in his uniform, don't you think?"

"Yes, he does." Susan took the photograph that Mrs. Gerty was passing to her. The boy in the silver frame smiled up at her. He had a cheerful face. Not like his mother's. But now, as Mrs. Gerty set it back on the mantelpiece, Susan understood that sometimes there were reasons to feel sorry for people who seemed to take pleasure in being unkind. The older she grew, the more complicated life seemed.

42

Was it Imagination?

When Dad entered the room a while later he found the two of them sitting side by side on an old weather-beaten sofa with Mrs. Gerty turning the flimsy pages of a photo album. The two of them started when suddenly he appeared before them.

"Mr Thomas!"

"Thank you for keeping an eye on my daughter," Mrs. Gerty.

"My pleasure. It's just a shame we didn't have the opportunity before."

"We create our opportunities, Mrs. Gerty."

"Not always, Mr. Thomas," she replied, closing the album and hugging it close to her chest. "Sometimes they are made for us."

In the reception hall a female police officer was waiting to ask Susan some questions.

"It's fine, Dad" she said, as he tried to field the officer off. "I'm ready to talk."

Up in the room Susan described everything in detail and Dad listened with a look of amazement as she explained exactly what had happened. The only aspect she left out was the view she had seen through the misty window almost two weeks earlier. No one would have believed her anyway.

'You've been tremendously helpful," said the officer, flipping her notebook shut and slipping it into her chest pocket. "Someone will inform you as soon as we have any news of the boy. His name is Kuba, by the way."

"Well, well," Dad said after showing her out. "This isn't exactly the holiday I had planned, what with sunstroke and now this. Do you regret coming?"

Susan thought for a while about Steven and Miss Lister, about Mr. Harry and Mr. Price, about Lee and his Nan, about the mouse episode and now the message in the bottle and then told him truthfully that she wasn't sorry.

But what of the views through the misty windows? Susan was quite certain that what had taken place on the beach was exactly what she had seen in the games room. She was equally sure that the house she'd seen through the top landing window would be exactly what Lee's Nan's new house would look like and that she would give in to Lee's desire for a swimming pool. Of that, she had no doubt.

Of the sad little Mexican girl and the balloon she was not so convinced. Somehow the little porcelain Josanya wasn't quite it. There was something more to it, she believed.

What Susan could not grasp was this. If the pictures were, indeed, linked to reality, as it was obvious to her now that they were, why her? She was just a typical thirteen year old girl from a standard English home, albeit with strict parents. Of course, her teachers were often telling her she had enough imagination for the whole class. Maybe that was the key? Maybe she *had* imagined it.

"A penny for your thoughts!" Dad said.

"No way!" Susan said. "They are worth a pound at least!"

"I see you haven't lost your sense of humour!" Dad exclaimed. "That's good!"

"I think I'm going to need it for when Peter comes barging in," Susan said ruefully. "I can hear his poem now

My sis, Suz is a hero.
I'm proud of her, I am!
If you ever need her — call her!
She'll come running if she can!

"I can see that writing poetry runs in the family," Dad told her. "You've been giving Peter some tips, by the sounds of things!"

"He doesn't need any help," Susan began, only to be interrupted by a sharp rap at the door, and when Dad answered it, there were two policemen asking for, of all people, her.

"You'll be glad to know that the boy from the beach has regained consciousness. While the doctors can't tell if there's any permanent damage they are hopeful that, having come to so swiftly he may actually have chance of a full recovery."

Finding it difficult to catch her breath Susan buried her face in her hands and listened as the police officer continued, tears of relief trickling down her cheeks.

"His parents are flying into Bristol late this evening and they've specifically asked if they can meet the girl who saved their son's life. How about tomorrow morning at about eleven? We'll bring them here from the hospital."

"I think that would be fine, officer," Dad said, and Susan agreed, even though it seemed strange that they would want to see someone they didn't know.

"Good. We won't keep you any longer. Just thought you might like the good news."

The door burst open and in rushed Peter, straight into the arms of one of the departing policemen followed very closely by Kathy and Mum, who was holding Anna's hand. The little girl was so shy that she had to be coaxed into the room.

"What did the police say?" Mum asked.

"He's regained consciousness."

"My thith ith a hero! My thith ith a hero! Peter yelled, jumping round the room in delight.

Dad and Susan burst out laughing, which was just what was needed.

"Actually, Peter, it should be "heroine" since your sister is a girl!" Dad explained.

Susan realized her dad hadn't corrected her when she'd made the same mistake earlier.

"A private joke? Have I missed something?" asked a very bemused Mum.

"I'll tell you later. For once I happen to agree wholeheartedly with our youngest."

Kathy went over to her sister and put her arms round Susan. "Well done!" she whispered.

Peter's hug was so much like a rugby tackle, that Susan was winded for a second. Finally, it was Mum's turn. Once the family had congratulated Susan she came face to face with the little blond girl who turned out to be Anna who flushed with pleasure when Susan explained how her grandfather had helped save a boy. She did not mention her role in all this because, after all, she had only done what was necessary. Still, she found that she was exhausted, and when Dad and the others went to tea, she was glad enough to sink into a dreamless sleep.

43

Cameras Galore

"Shhh, she'th thtill athleep!" Susan heard Peter say.

"We won't disturb her then," Mum warned him in a whisper. "If you can't fall asleep again pick up all your toys and put them in your bag. I'll ask Daddy to take them down to the car when we go down for breakfast."

"Right, Mum. Hey, Kathy have a look out of the window! Mr. Chrith ith back with the camera crew."

Susan listened as her brother and sister tiptoed over to the window. She felt her bed jolt as they pulled the curtain back a little and heard Kathy's stifled gasp.

"Wait till Susan sees," her sister whispered.

Susan didn't want to open her eyes. She was disappointed that she had missed her last evening in Teignmouth. Knowing that once the family realised she was awake, they'd only have a couple of hours left before getting in the car, she decided to keep her eyes tightly shut.

"What is the Devon News van here for and the Taunton Press?" Kathy continued in a whisper.

"Maybe Thuthan will be on TV!"

"Or maybe they're all here for Steven's Mum's book signing."

"Let'th go down and thee."

When she heard the door click behind them, Susan lifted herself up on her elbows and lifted the bottom corner of the curtain.

"Flipin' heck."

"What is it, Susan?"

"Camera crews – everywhere."

Susan was nervous and excited and terrified all rolled into one. What if Peter had been right? What if she *was* going to be on TV? No, it couldn't be. Kathy's version was far more likely.

"Look at this everyone!" Kathy cried, charging into the room. "Susan you've got to wake up – Oh, you are! Look! It's you!"

Sure enough, it was. There, on page one of the local newspaper, under the main heading.

DORSET GIRL SAVES POLISH YOUTH FROM CERTAIN DEATH

It was a full description of what had happened the previous day, a school photo of Kuba and a picture of Susan and Mr. Harry sitting on the back of the ambulance. It wasn't the best shot but it was definitely her. The story continued on page seven and when Susan turned to it she was in for a pleasant surprise. Someone had taken a shot of Miss Lister as she was walking down the promenade the previous morning in the company of the girl who had later saved the Polish boy.

"Is that you, too?" asked Kathy and Susan flushed with pleasure as she saw Miss Lister's scarf round her neck. With the elegant hair style it really did make for a very pretty picture.

Snatching the paper away Kathy bounded over to Mum and Dad's bed to show them the picture. "See Steven's mum."

"So the paparazzi has been at it again," Dad said. "Poor Miss Lister. I'm sure she's sick and tired of them."

"It's not just Miss Lister," Kathy told him. "They didn't put the picture in because of her this time. It's because of Susan."

"My word – so it is!" Dad exclaimed. "Mary, you'd better have a look at this!"

They all climbed onto the big double bed and Dad read the story out loud from beginning to end.

"Are you ready for the cameras, Susan?" he said when he had finished. "It isn't every day that somewhere peaceful like Teignmouth has a boy saved from near death!"

"Do you really think they'll want to talk to me?"

"I have absolutely no doubt whatsoever. I suggest you go and do whatever it is that women do to make themselves more beautiful."

"But I've packed all my clothes!"

"Can't you wear what you had on yesterday?"

"Mum, the T-shirt's got brown stains all over it from the sand. I wish I could ask Miss Lister for help. But I can't. The cameras might all be for her and I'd feel really stupid."

"What about borrowing Mum's blouse?" asked Kathy.

"Hey, Kathy that's a brilliant idea. You wouldn't mind, would you Mum?"

"On this occasion, no, I wouldn't mind. Put your white T-shirt under it because it's rather see-through."

The only thing I've got that would go with it are my jeans" Susan groaned as she gently removed Mum's delicate, see-through blouse from its hanger.

"I'm going downthtairth if you're drething up," said Peter crossing his arms and humphing.

When Kathy suggested that she wear her hair loose for a change, Susan let it fall over her shoulders and, looking in the mirror, was pleased with the result. Perhaps Steven's mother, by example, had taught both she and Kathy the sort of lesson they would never forget.

44

Miss Lister Missing

There was pandemonium in the lobby. A long table had been set up along one side with two microphones in the middle. Under the table were sealed cardboard boxes which Susan guessed contained Miss Lister's book. Mr. Chris was giving directions to two boys who were assembling a display board behind the table. A third had rolls of paper tucked under his arm which looked like they might be posters. Susan was dying to have a peek. Steven's mum was nowhere to be seen and Mr. Chris was looking anxious.

"Hello!" he said. "Susan, isn't it? You haven't seen Liz, I mean Miss Lister, have you? She should have been here ten minutes ago and she's usually spot on."

"No, I'm sorry I haven't," Susan told him. "Maybe she's in the dining room. I'll go and check if you like?"

"Thank you," he said, and as Susan went to peek in the next room, she heard him call out, "No boys! To your left. Back five, no ten centimetres. Stop! Yes, perfect. Right. Get those posters up, pronto! We've only got forty-five minutes left. Damn. Where is she? Colin, can you use someone else to get the sound levels right?"

"She's not there," she told him, skipping across the floor.

"Look, do me a favour. Colin over there . Yes, the one waving at me. Well, he's got to do a sound check. Be a dear, Susan. Just sit on that chair and say "testing – testing 1-2-3" for us, will you?"

"Sure!" Sitting down she tapped the microphones like she'd seen on the films. "Testing – testing – 1-2-3"

"That's good. Now the other one!"

"Testing – testing 1-2-3" Susan repeated it until Colin nodded and did a thumbs up sign."

"Thanks kid. We're all set Chris!"

Susan walked round the table and noticed another cameraman peering through the main door.

"I think someone's looking for you, Mr. Chris."

"Oh, them. No, we didn't invite them. They're not here for us."

Susan felt herself blush. And then it happened. The main door opened and a very smart woman, holding a cordless microphone, walked in and straight up to Susan.

"Susan? Susan Thomas?" she said crisply. "Would you mind stepping out where the light is better. We'd like to ask you about Kuba?"

Before knowing how, and certainly not recalling that she'd actually agreed, Susan found herself out on the top step, facing reporters, all of whom seemed to be hurling a barrage of questions at her until the woman who had accompanied her outside held up her hand.

"One at a time," she told them, and started the ball rolling with a simple "What can you tell us about yesterday?"

Susan begin to tell them about the afternoon and about the accident, and although she did not raise her voice, everyone listened intently, including the reporters at the back of the crowd. When she described the horror she felt on seeing Kuba slowly disappear, she heard the cameras begin to click, and saw that many of the women were silently weeping.

When she finished a young reporter from one of the local stations asked if she knew how Kuba was.

"I only know that he regained consciousness yesterday evening."

"What will you say to his mother and father when they arrive?" yet another reporter asked.

"I don't know yet." Susan replied feeling suddenly nervous at the thought of meeting Kuba's parents.

Mum and Dad had come to stand behind her on the hotel steps.

"What do your parents say about what happened yesterday?" a reporter asked.

"We're very, very proud of her," Dad replied, and then, as reporters focused on her parents, Susan turned aside to find Miss. Lister coming toward her with a frantic look in her lovely eyes.

"What happened?" she demanded.

"There was an accident on the beach," Susan told her. "A boy almost died when the hole he was digging gave in."

Miss Lister went strangely pale, but didn't have time to respond before Mr. Chris took her by the arm and escorted her back inside the hotel. Only then did it occur to Susan that she must have thought it was Steven.

45

The book Signing

Susan sat down opposite Miss Lister.

"I'd like to buy a copy of your book, Miss Lister."

"Sorry, Susan. I can't sell you one."

"Why not?"

"Because, for you there's a special one. The first at a book signing should always receive a free copy. Wouldn't you agree, Mr. Chris?" Leaning across the table she spoke softly. "If you'd been the twenty-fifth you would still have a received a special one. Just promise me one thing."

"Of course!"

"Reality is not always what it appears and fiction can sometimes be more real the reality itself."

"Pardon?"

"Someday you'll understand. Find yourself a quiet spot away from the crowds when you open my book."

"All right" said Susan, not understanding a word she'd just heard but trusting that the glamorous lady in front of her knew what she was talking about."

By now the cameras were fixed on Miss Lister, and the hotel guests, who had willingly followed Susan back into the lobby, had been joined by tourists from the town and were busily organizing themselves in good old British tradition, in an orderly queue.

Mr. Chris took the cloth off the notice board and the books and a murmur went through the crowd.

Susan felt a chill go up her spine.

The title of Miss Lister's book was "MIST ON THE WINDOW".

46

Kuba's Parents Arrive

It was a strange feeling, very like what Susan had felt when she had seen the mist on the window with her own eyes. What could it mean? Had Miss Lister seen the same thing? She knew she had to read the book, to find out what was happening. But on the other hand, she wasn't sure that she wanted to. It was all too mysterious. But she did know that she wouldn't be able to simply put *Mist on the Window* on a shelf without ever discovering what it was about. She had no choice but to look. Leaving Miss Lister to sign her book she wandered down the corridor and sat nervously in the bay window.

Gingerly turning the book over on her lap, she looked at the cover.

Teignmouth promenade, the family, her misty boy. Even the misty window and the hand. If she were a real artist she might have drawn a similar picture to describe her own Teignmouth holiday. Just inside the cover was the puzzling sentence that Miss Lister had spoken back in the lobby,

Reality is not always what it appears and fiction can sometimes be more real the reality itself. From the Author to the Main Character.

Slowly, very slowly Susan opened to page one.

1

Mr. Kramer Locked Up

"You didn't?" said Kathy, her eyes open as wide as Mum's new dinner plates.

"I did!" answered Susan, proudly sticking out her chin.

"You really did it?" asked Kathy, awestruck as usual by her older sister's courage. "I wish I had been there. What did he say?"

Susan chuckled as she remembered. "He had just sort of spluttered and muttered something about seeing the headmistress!"

But this was exactly what had happened! How could Miss Lister have known that? Perhaps she had seen the mist on the window here at the hotel, but this was all about Susan's life before she had come here.

"Susan? Susan?" she heard Mum cry. "Oh, there you are. A policeman has just arrived to see if you're ready and I asked him if you could have ten minutes. I have a feeling you haven't had anything to eat." Mum reached up and tucked Susan's hair behind her ear – a habit she'd had since as long as Susan could remember. "That's better! Am I right?"

"Yes, you're right. No. I didn't have breakfast. But it wasn't exactly my fault."

"I'm not blaming anyone, Susan. I'm just here to ask if you fancy a quiet cup of tea and a piece of toast away from the crowds. Nanny found me a minute ago and said that the couple from room twenty-one left half an hour ago and she'd set up their table in the corner. Remember the one? You children always wished we could have it because it was hidden away behind screens like a secret place."

"A cup of tea sounds lovely," Susan said, thankful for the chance to escape from everyone and the mystery. "But I don't think my tummy will cope with toast."

"Come on then. Fortunately you chose here to hide. At least we don't have to try barging our way through the mob outside."

The tea break was just what Susan needed and she would have liked to stay there longer but Nanny came in before long with the news that Kuba's parents had just arrived.

"Here goes!" she said, straightening her shoulders absolutely determined to appear calm, though certainly not feeling it.

"You'll be fine. You were so composed in front of the cameras this morning. Dad and I were so proud. Here, why don't you give me the book?"

"No, it's okay," Susan said, clutching it to her. "It'll be good to have something to hold onto." One thing was certain. She wasn't about to let anyone else read what Miss Lister had written ... at least, not until she'd worked out what it all meant.

One of the policemen pushed his way through the crowd and asked the people to make a way through for Kuba's parents.

"Get them to stand on the stairs so we can get some shots," someone shouted over the din.

The couple who came toward her, holding out their hands, were younger than Susan's parents, and rather smartly dressed. They were both beaming, no doubt with relief, and the woman embraced her. A young tourist guide materialized to translate as they stood on the stairs to let photographers take their shots.

It was all so forced and unnatural. Susan caught herself thinking it would have been better to have met Kuba's mum and dad privately in the dining room. It was clear that the woman had been crying for a long time, but she did a good job at remaining calm in front of the cameras. Even when the microphone was shoved in her face she managed to keep her composure, and according to the translator, said that she and her husband would always be in Susan's debt and that she hoped that one day she and her family might be their guests in Poland.

Susan didn't have to say anything on this occasion except "Thank you" when they handed her the biggest bouquet of roses she'd even seen. It was so big that she disappeared from sight behind it. Fortunately, one of the hotel guests had the sense to take it from her so that she was visible again.

A doctor, who had been asked to escort Kuba's parents, was asked to give an update on the boy's condition and Susan listened with a growing sense of relief as he explained how amazed the hospital staff were by the speed of his recovery.

"None of us expected to ever take part in something so remarkable," he said. "This lad shouldn't even be alive but thanks to some quick thinking and help from the services I am able to inform you that we are hopeful for a full recovery. But if you will excuse us now. I need to be getting back to my patient and I know Kuba's mum and dad are eager to be back with their son."

The hotel resounded with thunderous applause and people moved with the doctor, the police and the young couple out through the door into the street where they waved farewell. The reporters packed up as quickly as they could in order to get to the hospital to follow the story and the hotel became strangely quiet.

Just as Susan picked up the bouquet which was lying on the stairs. Nanny appeared at her side.

"Here, Sweetie. I'll take those for you and wrap them for you so that you can take them home."

"No, Nanny. I'd like you and Mrs. Gerty to have them. All except this one," and she pulled out one single red rose. "This one's for Miss Lister."

And when they told her that Steven's mum was in the dining room, Susan hurried there at once. Because, along with everything else, she now knew that there was a special bond between them, although precisely what it really was she might, she realised, never find out.

47

The Mystery Deepens

Miss Lister, clearly deep in thought, was sitting in the dining room, holding a mug of tea in both hands. When Susan spoke to her, she jumped.

"Sorry I startled you," Susan said. "I just wanted to say goodbye."

Miss Lister took the rose that Susan was offering her. "Oh, thank you, Susan," she said. "It's lovely. Steven asked me to say goodbye, as well. I know he would have wanted to say thank you for being such good friends to him this holiday."

"Miss Lister?"

"Yes, Susan?"

"I um – wanted to ask..."

"Yes, I thought you'd have questions, although I'm afraid I don't think I'm going to have the answers for you. It was the accident that got me thinking. It was you who saved the boy, just like Susan in the book."

"Really!" Susan said, her mind in a whirl.

"I think you will find there are far more coincidences than just the accident, Susan."

"You mean, like my French teacher?"

Steven's mum looked astonished. "Are you telling me that even *that* is true? My goodness! How much have you managed to read?"

"Nothing else. Only about me, I mean Susan, shutting the French teacher in the cupboard."

"So, maybe there'll be differences too. Will you write and tell me?"

"Yes. All right." Susan said, excited at the prospect of being in contact with Miss Lister.

"Where's your book?" Miss Lister asked her. "Don't worry. I just want to write my address inside the back cover.

"Will you write another book?" Susan asked her.

"I've already started the second. But I had to stop because I can't work out what decision Susan is going to make."

"What's it going to be about?"

"That would be telling. Listen, tell you what. Read *Mist in the Window* first and then write to me, okay? And

Susan? Don't expect to find all the answers in the book. Like in life, not everything can always be explained."

Susan knew, quite suddenly, that she was right. Some things can never be explained. In a way, that was the magic of childhood, and Steven's mother had taught her that perhaps that need never change.

"Excuse me, ladies," Mr. Chris announced, appearing in the doorway. "Liz, the boys have almost finished packing up. How long do you need to get ready?"

"Give me twenty minutes." Miss Lister said, standing and holding out her arms to Susan who hugged her tight.

Susan found her family all waiting for her in the reception hall, suitcases and bags lined up ready to go. It was time for them to leave. But first she had one more thing to do. With a word to her father, she bolted up the stairs and tiptoed into their room for the very last time. Bright sunshine poured through the windows. How she would miss this room. She stayed for a moment then walked back out into the corridor, leaving the door open a fraction. It seemed too final to close it somehow.

Mrs. Gerty was standing at the corner of the stairs.

"I'm not good at goodbyes, so I thought I would catch you up here," she said. "I don't know what to give young ladies, but I thought you might like this to remember us all by."

The postcard she handed Susan had an old, faded black and white photograph of the hotel on it.

Susan threw her arms round her then. She had learned so much on this last holiday to Teignmouth, and one of them was that, not only were things not always what they seemed, but neither were people.

"I'm ready," she said as she returned to her family.

"Good thing. We've been waiting for abtholutely ageth!"

Peter ducked to avoid being cuffed around the ear by Dad.

48

Goodbye. Or is it Hello?

Nanny held the door open for the family and hugged each in turn.

"You keep your eye on these three special children, Mrs. Thomas," she said. "I would hate to hear of them going off the rails like so many do nowadays."

Mum and Dad walked out of the hotel, pausing at the bottom step to look back and then at each other before heading for the car park.

Peter wanted to beat Kathy to the car but she glanced at Susan and declined the offer of yet another challenge.

"No, Peter," she said. "You go on and I'll wait for Susan."

Nanny held her arms open and smothered Susan in an affectionate bear hug.

"Susan, my pet. I've given your dear parents my address. If you ever need someone to talk to, you can always write. I'm good at keeping secrets and I have a feeling you have at least one you may need to share with someone one day."

"Thank you, Nanny," Susan said, wondering whether she would ever be able to share her secrets with anyone.

"What did she say to you, Susan?" asked Kathy inquisitively.

Susan turned her head away. She knew that now was *not* the time to do any explaining.

"Gosh, you don't tell me anything anymore," Kathy said when Susan did not reply. "You haven't even shown me the ornament you got when you went with Miss Lister. And you promised!"

"Sorry, Kathy. Quite a lot has happened since then and I completely forgot. I'll show you when we get home. Okay?"

"Hmmm. Why was Nanny talking to you about secrets?"

"So, you *did* hear!"

"Only the word 'secret'."

"Forget it, Kathy!"

"You're such a spoil sport, Susan. You're no fun anymore."

"Maybe I'll tell you one day. But not today. Please, not today."

By the time they got to the car Kathy was in a real huff.

"In you get, all of you!" Dad said, and Susan could tell that he was as upset about leaving as she was.

Resisting the urge to go over to the wall and have one more look, she got into the car and rested her head against the window, wanting desperately to cry. But she had no tears left and in any case she didn't want anyone telling her not to be sad about leaving Teignmouth. She *was* sad. And that was that.

When Dad turned the car round and carefully pulled out onto Den Promenade, Susan caught sight of Nanny, Mrs. Gerty and Miss Lister all standing together, gazing out of her misty window, waving goodbye.

As they rounded the corner Susan reached down for Miss Lister's book. She knew that she'd promised to find a place alone when she read. Kathy, still in a bad mood, was sitting with her back to Susan, discussing with Peter which car game they would play first. And since Dad was busy asking Mum which way she would prefer to go home, Susan felt alone enough to open the cover.

Flicking through the book she went straight to the chapter entitled "The Mouse". It was, she found, as if she was reading her own diary. She found the description of the mist on the top landing and then read the account of Peter's toe being bitten by a crab, then she hurriedly turned the pages until she got to the last chapter to read how Susan ended her stay in Teignmouth.

A few pages from the end Susan noticed that there was a view through a misty window that *she* hadn't personally experienced.

"Susan peered through the glass and saw a quaint, Spanish style chapel. There were hundreds of people milling around outside and she imagined she could hear laughter. On one of the walls behind the crowds she read the words "FBC invites you to Modesto" painted in bright colours on an enormous poster. As she pressed her nose against the misty window she squinted. There in the corner, just to the right of the church was her very own misty boy, smiling at the camera.

Susan's heart leapt. At least that was how it felt. Was Miss Lister telling her about the future, as accurately as she had described the past? Was she really going to see her Misty boy again?

"Dad, I need the loo," said Peter crossing his legs and biting his bottom lip.

"There's a lay-by in about two miles. I'll be able to stop then."

"Maybe we can tell them then, Darly?"

"Can't it wait till we get home?

"No! No! Tell uth now!" Peter said excitedly.

When the lay-by came into sight Dad slowed down and pulled over.

"Very well," Dad said, grinning. "Susan, pass me my briefcase please. You see, just before we left Mr James told me that there is no doubt that The hotel is going to be converted into flats this autumn. So a chapter in the Thomas family's life has come to an end. BUT before you all burst into tears, I have a surprise. Next summer, why don't we treat ourselves to a trip to California?"

He handed back a folder with a picture of a quaint, Spanish styled chapel on the front. And there he was, standing right in front! There was Lee, her very own misty boy, smiling at the camera!

Or was he, Susan thought, smiling at her?

Thanks to the people of Teignmouth, who made my return after thirty-five years a most magic moment, particularly to Tony and Pat Hotham and Don and Kathy Bissell for allowing me back into "The Hotel" and to the Ferryman, for giving me 'freedom of the ferry.'

To Wade Collectors Club for giving permission to use the name Wade Whimsies. ©Wade Ceramics Ltd.

To Magdalena Pytka, for her painstaking work in the illustrations

To Mary Linn Roby for her invaluable help with the editing

With especial thanks to Mum, Kathie and Peter for letting me use so many real details – and to Dad, of course

About the Author

Susan Thomas-Czarnecki was born in Southampton, England in 1965. Educated in Dorchester, she moved to California at the age of seventeen, returning to England two years later to study Theology at London Bible College.

After three years teaching Religious Studies in Norwich she moved again, but this time East, settling in Poland, where she lives today with her family and where she runs an English language school.

Lightning Source UK Ltd.
Milton Keynes UK
10 April 2010

152593UK00001B/3/P